ALPHA'S REVENGE

A WEREWOLF SHIFTER ROMANCE (ROYAL ALPHA WOLVES CLUB BOOK 3)

CATHERINE STINE

Konjur Road Press
Forays into Fictional Magic

Alpha's Revenge

A Werewolf Shifter Romance
(Royal Alpha Wolves Club Book 3)

Synopsis:

Wayland - a heartbroken furious alpha.
Stormy - a forbidden childhood crush revisited.
Wayland's out to avenge the murder of his mate
and royal Leblanc dynasty by a rival Tundra, Thorn.
But he didn't plan on falling for Thorn's sister, Stormy.
Pursuing this star-crossed Juliet to his Romeo might cost Wayland and
Stormy their lives.

***

For news of books, events and sales subscribe to Catherine's newsletter or
visit her at catherinestine.com

GROUP PROLOGUE

$\mathcal{W}$ ayland, Dorian, Alec and Tobias

"ANY IDEA WHY WE'RE HERE?" Dorian grumbled under his breath as he found a spot in the back room of the Lazy Moon.

Looking around the crowded bar full of alpha wolves from all around the world, he was sure whatever the reason for calling them together wasn't a good one. Ever their careful leader, Tobias normally tried to avoid filling a space with too many shifters. One wrong look could cause a wolf to slip off leash. Especially these wolves.

Never in Dorian's entire time as a member of the Royal Alpha Wolves Club had he ever been summoned to a mandatory meeting of all the royal packs. There were pack representatives from every corner of the world here tonight. Something was up.

To say the mood was tense was an understatement. The

Lazy Moon was one spark away from exploding. And that made it the last place Dorian wanted to be. He'd had enough violence in his life lately, but as he was the last of the Calhoun bloodline, he had no choice but to attend.

"How much do you want to bet Tobias is about to add another ridiculous law to the Club rule book?" Alec muttered crossing his arms beside Dorian.

Dorian glanced at the smug shifter. He wouldn't exactly call Alec St. James a friend, more like a drinking buddy. But in this room, Alec was the closest thing to a friend Dorian had and he needed at least one wolf guarding his back if shit hit the fan. And if he were being honest, Alec would always be Dorian's first choice in a fight.

Alec St. James loved a good bar brawl more than anyone Dorian knew. Built like a boxer, the arrogant alpha had the skills to back it up. When he wasn't chasing tail, he was in the ring.

Alec wasn't in Dorian's pack, but they roamed the same territory and therefore belonged to the same local chapter of the Club. And even though Alec was from a much wealthier pack of royals than Dorian, he often saw Alec hanging around the Lazy Moon biker bar.

The young shifter seemed to enjoy slumming it, or maybe he just enjoyed the action the nefarious location was famous for.

Lazy Moon was known to attract women who were looking for a good time with a bad boy. Though it was against pack law for shifters to reveal their true nature to humans, there were no rules against fucking them. And Alec enjoyed bragging about how many notches he had in his bedposts—human and shifter alike.

"I don't think this is about rules," Dorian replied.

There weren't a lot of rules set by the Club: don't reveal

yourself to humans, no unsanctioned kills and never mess with another wolf's mate. Easy enough. Or at least it was for Dorian. Alec on the other hand walked the line when it came to flirting with spoken for females.

"Maybe you finally bedded the wrong wolf," Dorian teased. "This could be the stage for your execution."

Alec laughed. "Are you forgetting who I am?" He arched an eyebrow. "I'm a St. James. We're practically untouchable."

"Practically," Dorian stressed. "Not completely." Being that Dorian was also a single alpha male, he and Alec often found themselves prowling the same territory for females. That had led to more than a few disputes over shared bottles of whiskey at Lazy Moon.

Most wolves wouldn't have been able to settle such things so civilly, but Dorian wasn't most wolves. His heart was never really in it when it came to pursuit of a mate. How could it be when his heart already belonged to the one woman he couldn't have.

He shook the agonizing thought away and tried to refocus on his hostile surroundings. Alec was still on his right, getting more than a few well-deserved glares from some of the other alphas. Say what you will about Alec's womanizing ways, but Dorian admired him. It was hard not to respect someone with as much style and balls as Alec St. James. Especially for his age. His family may have a history of being womanizing pricks, but Dorian had always believed in second chances.

"Maybe the Club is just hard up for dues," Dorian added sarcastically.

Alec snorted a laugh, but it was cut off by the deep tenor of another voice.

"It's nothing that trivial," Wayland added, walking up beside them.

Alec's mouth snapped shut and Dorian held his breath as the legendary alpha stopped next to them. His jaw muscles clenched as he surveyed the scene. The scent of dominance coming off the large male was stifling.

Everyone knew Wayland's family and the tragedy that had befallen them. The fact that he hadn't gone on a killing spree that eradicated every wolf in the territory spoke of his superior restraint. But the intense iciness of his glare made one wonder if he was just biding his time.

It had been a major coup when Wayland Leblanc joined the Club's Louisiana chapter. Just about every pack in the country could be traced back to Wayland's royal bloodline. But then again, that was probably why his entire pack had been slaughtered recently. Having that kind of notoriety and power would put a bull's-eye on anyone's back.

Dorian was searching for something to say to the massive alpha when Tobias took the podium. His voice echoed through the room, calling the milling shifters to attention.

"Brothers, thank you for coming on such short notice. I'm sorry to have been so vague and mysterious, but as you know, we can never be too careful." Tobias let his eyes settle on Wayland while his words sank in. "I know your time is precious, so I'll cut right to it. We are a dying breed. I know this is nothing new to you, but the Royal Alpha Wolves Club was formed centuries ago to protect our kind. And until recently, we've been successful.

"The fall of the Leblanc pack was a major blow to shifters everywhere. It is the reason for this meeting. Such acts of violence cannot be allowed to stand. The damage from pack wars and the increasing encroachment of humans has dwindled our numbers and territory to dangerous numbers.

"That's a problem for the Louisiana territory!" someone shouted.

Tobias didn't miss a beat. "This is not an isolated event.

This is an epidemic. Our numbers are decreasing globally, not just here. But I have a plan and if we work together we can ensure the werewolf species will not stop here. That's why I've called you all here," he paused dramatically. "With the blessing of the council, I'm enacting a new decree."

Alec huffed. "Told ya, more laws."

"We must preserve our race," Tobias continued. "In order to do so it has been decided by the council that all unmated alphas from each royal bloodline must find a mate and produce an heir within the year."

Uproar erupted from the crowd as shifters shouted their discontent, but somehow Tobias reclaimed his audience. "I know the timeframe is harsh, but it is no harsher than the reality that our race is dying. Let me be clear. If we don't do something to preserve our kind, the end of the wolves will be upon us and that is something I cannot accept."

"A year?" Alec muttered. "Is he joking?"

"Oh, come on. You bring home a new chick every night. You'll have no problem," Dorian teased.

Alec narrowed his eyes. "Women aren't the problem, it's the whole settling down bit I'm not into. I'm a royal for fuck's sake. Side action is my right! I'm not letting some old fleabag tell me my days of meaningless sex are over."

"Relax," Dorian added. "It's not like he can really reinforce it."

"I wouldn't be so sure," Wayland added.

Dorian studied Wayland. "What do you know?"

"Nothing more than you. But this wouldn't be the first time harsh measures were used to ensure our survival."

"What do you mean?" Dorian asked.

Before Wayland could answer, Tobias spoke again. "I know the time constraints aren't ideal, but we must do what is necessary to survive, which brings me to my next point. Any alpha that doesn't produce a new heir by next year will forfeit their royal lineage and be reassigned to a pack that has proved the strength of its bloodline."

If Dorian thought the room had been a powder keg, Tobias's words provided the spark. Pandemonium erupted as alphas raged and shouted profanities. Some were so indignant they lost hold of their wolves, shifting and turning the crowded room into a ruckus of fur, gnashing jaws and bloodlust.

In Tobias's haste to preserve his dwindling population of royal shifters, it seemed he'd forgotten to take into account that his new decree would cause more harm than good.

How the hell had he not anticipated this?

Wolves were a proud species. Ancestry and family meant everything to them, especially the royal lines. The alphas here would do anything to preserve their bloodlines. Openly threatening them like this was practically an act of war.

Dorian saw the Brazil pack's leader in front of Alec get shoved hard by a wolf in mid-shift. Thinking it was Alec who affronted him, the guy turned swinging, but Dorian anticipated the blow, pulling Alec out of the way in the nick of time.

"Shit! Thanks," Alec said, watching the burly Brazilian shifter who'd been gunning for him crash into someone else.

But the reprieve was short lived. One enraged wolf replaced another as Alec and Dorian did their best to fight them off. If it hadn't been for Wayland jumping in to save their asses, Dorian would've had to shift to hold his own. But the last thing he wanted to do was add more chaos to the already vicious scene.

Together the three of them formed an unspoken agreement to fight together, watching each other's backs as enraged wolves rebelled against the very club that was supposed to protect them.

The Royal Alpha Wolves Club was an ancient organization formed to protect werewolves and the secrets of their species. They had chapters all over the world that offered safe houses for wolves in need and rules to keep local packs in line. The Lazy Moon was the Club's headquarters in the Louisiana territory. It was supposed to be a safe place for all shifters. But Tobias had just turned it into a war zone.

Normally, the Lazy Moon operated as a secret shifter club hiding in plain sight. It operated as a biker bar, which was the perfect cover since shifters usually resembled the Alpha male type that assembled as such places. It was easy for shifters to blend in among the groups of rowdy bikers that frequented the bar. And the remote location ensure that the clientele was mostly shifters, but remaining open to the public was good cover and prevented people from getting too suspicious at what went on there.

The Alpha Wolves Club hadn't always been that way, but what started as an ancient order housed in palaces and fortresses had to be modernized. Today the Lazy Moon was one of the Club's many safe havens that operated around the world offering a sanctuary for any werewolf in need. It was the reason Dorian had survived the brutal attack on his family and he would never forget that, but this was crossing the line.

Deadlines for mates?

Enforced breeding?

Abolishing royal bloodlines?

A percussion whistle tore through the melee halting the violence long enough for Tobias and his council to regain control, but Dorian remained on high alert. Breathing hard, he glanced at Alec and Wayland to assess their injuries. If things went south, he needed to know their strengths. Relief surged through him as he realized they were relatively unscathed.

He shouldn't be surprised, the St. James and Leblanc

bloodlines were two of the strongest, right up there with his own, the Calhouns. But one thing they had that Dorian didn't was backup. Dorian was the last of his name. So if it came down to it, he would put himself first. Preserving the bloodline was paramount.

Tobias's voice boomed through the room again once the council regained order. "Don't fight each other. The goal is to create larger packs and stronger bloodlines. If all of you can deliver an heir, nothing has to change. So I suggest you stop fighting each other and focus on finding a mate. Time is wasting."

Alec nudged Dorian's shoulder. He didn't need to be told twice. He wanted to get out while he could. He caught Wayland's eye and nodded toward an exit. Outside the three alphas drank in the cool night air.

"So, this is really happening?" Alec said, pacing as he ran his hand through his thick hair.

"It seems so," Wayland replied.

"Shit!" Dorian muttered. "It's not that I don't understand the sentiment, but this wasn't the way to go about it."

"What's done is done," Wayland added.

Dorian grunted in frustration. But Wayland was right. Sticking around here and bitching wasn't going to do anything but get him in a fight he wasn't looking for. Instead, he stuck his hand out to Wayland. Considering this might be the last time he ever saw the wolf, he wanted to stay in his good graces. "Thanks for saving my ass back there. I'm Dorian, by the way."

Wayland's eyes sparked with recognition. "Calhoun?" Dorian nodded. "I'm sorry to hear about your pack," he replied.

"Me too," Dorian answered.

For a moment, Dorian wondered if he'd overstepped as

Wayland quietly studied him. But after a moment, Wayland said, "Thanks. If there's every anything I can do to help…"

"Same goes for me," Dorian said clasping the alpha's forearm.

"Well shit, if we're making vows then me too," Alec said sauntering closer to add his fist to the mix.

The three alphas shared a silent look before breaking apart to go their separate ways.

"Good luck," Dorian said.

"And good fortune," Wayland said finishing off the familiar farewell.

"And may I find more mates than all of you," Alec added.

Dorian smirked. "It's not a contest, Alec."

"The hell it isn't. Let's make it interesting. We each throw in ten grand, winner takes all."

Dorian huffed a laugh. "Too rich for my blood."

Alec frowned. "Really?"

"We're not all from the St. James fortune."

Undeterred Alec grinned. "Fine, a hundred bucks each. Just to make it fun."

Wayland gave Dorian a skeptical look, but he only shrugged.

"Ah come on," Alec begged. "Having to settle down is going to kill me. At least give me something to look forward to."

"And winning this bet will do that?" Wayland questioned.

Alec flashed that million-dollar smile. "Hey, I'm a simple guy. I like girls and money."

Wayland grinned. "Who doesn't?"

"Then it's a deal?" Alec asked, hope lighting his features.

"Fine, I'm in," Dorian said holding his hand out.

"Why not," Wayland said, joining him.

This time, after they shook hands Alec felt a bit less disheartened about the future. He briskly walked to his bike and kicked the motorcycle to life. As he sped away from the Lazy Moon, he let the roar of the engine drown out his worries. Tomorrow he'd worry about where the hell to start looking for a new mate. But tonight...well tonight he was going to do what he did best—find trouble.

* * *

Wayland

He slung his jacket on the lone hook on the back of his crappy apartment door. My how the mighty have fallen, he thought as he looked around the unfurnished apartment. He'd been in Louisiana for a while now, but he still hadn't been able to bring himself to unpack.

That would make things permanent. It would mean this was his life, and he wasn't sure he was ready to accept that yet. Leaving his territory in Canada had felt like the right move at the time. He couldn't be in that place, in that house, where the ghosts still lived.

Wayland was beginning to realize he couldn't outrun his heartbreak, no matter how far he traveled. He still couldn't quite figure out how to make himself whole again.

Everyone kept telling him it would take time. It had been a year since he lost them, and now thanks to Tobias's new decree it seemed Wayland was out of time.

But he wasn't ready yet. How could he be? He hadn't just lost his pack and royal status, but his mate and child. They were the only things that had actually mattered to him anyway. What good was all the wealth and power in the world if it wouldn't bring back the ones he loved?

Wayland knew Tobias's order was a tough one to swallow, but that's what being a leader was, making the tough decisions for the greater good. And even though he knew that's what this was he still couldn't do it. He couldn't chain himself to another mate.

First of all, it wouldn't be fair to whatever female he ended up with. He wasn't the alpha he used to be. Besides, no one would want this broken version of him that was left. He'd done an okay job of hiding how badly he was suffering, but if he had to invite someone in to get close enough to mate, they'd see the cracks. He didn't have the energy to hide his heartbreak twenty-four seven. That's why he spent most of his time holed up in this shitty apartment, plotting his revenge.

No, he couldn't drag someone else into his messed up life. He'd promised himself he wouldn't put anyone else in danger, and that's want being mated to him meant—danger.

Maybe he'd be off the hook. Maybe he was so damaged the mating bond wouldn't even stick if he tried. But that would mean being stripped of his bloodline and he had already lost too much.

Wayland owed the Royal Alpha Wolves Club everything. The ancient order took Wayland in when he had nothing. No pack, no territory, no other family. They fed him, gave him a home and helped him get back on their feet. They treated him like family and in return he would do anything for them. But not this.

There had to be another way.

When tragedy thrust him into the spotlight, Wayland had been forced to grow up fast. Not only had he lost his father and the rest of his pack in a brutal attack orchestrated by rival wolves, but Wayland's mate of a mere month had been slaughtered too.

As heir to the Leblanc pack, he'd been encouraged to marry young and produce his own heirs to preserve the royal line. He'd been mated with a young female named Sabine. Though their marriage had started as an alliance between packs, Wayland had quickly grown to love Sabine's gentle nature. But their time together was cut short by a brutal attack.

After Wayland's mate was slaughtered along with the rest of his pack, a letter Sabine had written him was uncovered. In it, she'd shared the joyful news that she was expecting.

Wayland shook away the memory. It still haunted him. He'd never really been the same since that day. But like with most things, death brings about the parts of life we're unprepared for. Since the tragic events that left him an heir without a pack, many things had changed for the Wayland. But thanks to the Club, he had survived then. He would survive this too.

The world could be a cruel place for werewolves who tried to live on their own. Being a shifter was a big secret to keep without the strength of a pack. Inevitably, the thing that caused lone wolves the most trouble was being forced to shift in order to protect themselves. It was most often the thing that got shifters killed or worse.

To most of the world, the existence of werewolves still remained hidden. Easily explained away as folklore and legend to the general public who had enough to worry about without adding another apex predator to their food chain. But there were small underground factions of humans who'd learned of the shifter community. Some were kind and chose to work with them, but most weren't.

But that was a worry for another day. Or perhaps another wolf. Because if Wayland didn't find a loophole to taking another mate he'd be giving up his legacy as werewolf royalty. His name would no longer be recognized in the shifter world.

As the only Leblanc heir, it felt unnatural to Wayland to turn tail and run. If there was any other way he'd take it. . . but his utmost duty was to preserve the royal bloodline.

Shifter numbers were dwindling as it was, and Wayland was determined not to let his family name end with him.

He took a good hard look at his reflection, his dark hair, hulking frame and emerald eyes. Leblanc eyes. He made his decision right then. He refused to lose anything more. It was time to fight back; time to fight for what was his.

CHAPTER 1

Wayland

WAYLAND PARKED the dinged-up silver minicamper in front of his apartment. The complex was adequate, with a front garden and a small swimming pool out back. It was his own crappy apartment he couldn't wait to get away from: the boxes he'd never unpacked, the photos he'd flipped face down, unable to look at or toss them. After the ultimatum the head of the royals club had doled out at the Lazy Moon this morning, Wayland bombed up to an RV lot near the Red River Park and bought the first used junker he'd seen.

"Moving out?" asked the turbaned old lady sitting on the bench out front, taking long draws of a skinny clay pipe and watching Wayland tear in and out with boxes.

"Going on an excursion," he said, hauling out his cooler full of root beer and bourbon.

The old lady shuffled the Tarot cards she kept in her lap

like a sleeping cat. She fanned them out. "One for the journey?"

He placed the cooler on the sidewalk and swiped a hand across his sweaty brow. This neighbor was a card reader, a crystal seller, and a maker of medicine bottles—whatever those were. Wayland had a warm spot for witches of any sort. Since he'd moved down here from Canada a year ago, they were some of the friendliest, down-to-earth folk around. "I'm game." He pulled one. Seven of Swords.

"Someone did you harm," she declared. His gut clenched in stinging fury. *Bull's-eye.*

She set her long pipe down on the bench and gazed at him. In her soft brown eyes and slow nod, it was clear she saw his pain.

"One more," she demanded. He didn't argue with wizened dames or witches. He pulled a second card and handed it to her. "Knight of Swords," she announced. "You're out for revenge."

He drew in a sharp breath. Scary accurate. "Duly noted. Thanks, ma'am," he said and picked up the cooler.

"Name's Nola Jaye. You?"

"Wayland Leblanc."

"Nice ring to it." As he went into the camper she called out, "Some excursion!"

You don't know the half of it. Thirty-eight freaking driving hours until I can begin to wreak my revenge for the acts that triggered my gory visions and insomnia.

He checked his backpack for his sleeping pills, snacks, and smartphone before he latched the camper door. Then he climbed into the driver's seat and gunned the motor, waving to the fortuneteller on his way out.

* * *

ON THE THIRD morning and the last leg to Canada, he filled the camper's tank with gas, wolfed down a blueberry scone and some beef jerky, and washed it all down with a root beer. He'd driven for fifteen long hours yesterday, but he was hell-bent on not wasting time to get up to Alberta, where his old Leblanc pack used to live by Ice Lake. Even with sleep remedies, the few hours he managed to get between driving stints were filled with bloody dreams.

Memories of the grisly slaughter of his entire Leblanc wolf pack by Thorn, a rival Tundra. Wayland and the Leblanc pack had fought back valiantly until they were sliced up by Thorn and his pack's nasty array of human cutlery.

The worst part was when he'd fallen on the ground, desperately weak and bleeding, and Thorn forced him to watch the slaughter of his mate, Sabine. Even now, the memory made him gag. Sabine's plush black fur had been matted with blood and her throat slashed—not by the werewolf's natural weapon, claws as long as sabers, but by cheater Thorn's human knife collection. What tortured Wayland even more was when he'd found out Sabine was pregnant with their baby. Many times after that, holed up in his dark apartment with his boxes of memories, he was tempted to end it all. But Wayland wasn't a quitter, and he longed for payback.

Thorn was head of the Tundra pack, and another royal wolf. Tundras and Leblancs had once shared the territory around Ice Lake—when they were cubs, they played together on the shores. Wayland remembered Thorn's pretty sister, Stormy and wrestling with her in the bramble. But all of that ended with Thorn's greed and his sadistic lust for control.

The feud escalated when Wayland's own father was in a deadly battle to protect his mate—Wayland's mother—from being abducted by Thorn's playboy father, Jagger. Wayland's dad pushed Thorn's father over a cliff near the Tundra hangout, World's Edge Bar. Although Thorn would use any excuse to throw others off the land, including the peaceful Windrunner wolves and the scruffy coyotes.

Wayland owed his life to the royal wolf shifters club in DeSoto Parish, in western Louisiana. They'd sent emergency emissaries to transport him south and nurse him back to health. He could barely stand to recall how close to death he was, hanging on a thread of agony.

Wayland drove the camper northward, blood pounding between his ears and his heart rattling against his badly-mended ribs. "My bones might've knit together but my mental scars will bleed until I get justice," he hissed. He had to park in an RV rest stop for twenty minutes to calm down.

* * *

THE HIGHWAY SIGN SAID ALBERTA. He'd made it!

In the campground, Wayland set out the folding chairs he'd scored on sale and was checking out the grill when he spotted a short blonde woman in the next lot, tending a pot over a cook fire. Cursing his bad luck, he slunk into his camper, shut the door and plunked on his mattress to rest before heading to World's Edge to stir up trouble. He wanted to be left alone in this campsite.

He was nowhere near ready to find a mate, no matter the ticking clock, and he needed time to clear his head. How would he ever get over Sabine's cruel slaughter? He doubted he'd ever have room in his heart for another baby after his first was brutally murdered, still inside his mate's womb. Fuck saving his royal title and the idiotic bet he agreed to with his club mates back in Louisiana. Sure, the royal shifter lines were fast disappearing, but was it his responsibility to repopulate the royals? He was fine with losing a bet to be the first to find a mate and make an heir.

What a stupid pissing contest.

Wayland tried to nap, but all he did was toss around and pull out the sheet corners. "I'll go to World's Edge for a drink," he mumbled aloud. "Just to scope it out and see if the Tundra even hang out there anymore."

He booted up, threw on a leather vest and raked a hand through his thick black hair, then checked his look in the mirror before brushing his teeth. The planes of his face were hardened from fatigue and stress. Sallow half-circles sat under his green eyes, his mouth was in a grim line and his five o-clock shadow had bristled into an unkempt beard. He'd shave the damn thing off later. "I look like hell warmed over." He sniggered. "But this isn't exactly a beauty pageant I'm going to."

Transforming to wolfish form to race through the forest, a momentary sense of freedom pulsed through him. These woods had been his heart, his boyish past. He loved the northern forests with their pines, stark stone ridges, rushing creeks, and brambles.

As he approached the World's Edge bar, his joy changed to anxiety, and he transformed again to human form. The last time he was here, he had crawled in, bleeding and barely alive, to phone the Louisiana chapter to ask for help.

Tundra shifters and other packs plus the occasional human could be found here. He glanced up at the blinking neon World's Edge sign, and had second thoughts about entering blindly. What if the place was brimming with Tundra? What if Thorn had heard about his arrival somehow and was already waiting there with his goon squad?

He took a few steps forward and paused again. Wayland knew he should figure out a detailed revenge plan so he wasn't outnumbered. On the other hand, he was hyped up and itching to start trouble. "Just on a small scale, first," he said under his breath. "Sense the mood. See which of my enemies is still around."

Wayland sucked it up and entered the bar. It was dark, but he could make out the old pool table by the far end and the row of stools along the bar. A couple of Tundra shifters sat there, talking and sipping their drinks. They turned to see who entered, and Wayland recognized the tall skinny guy with billowing white hair and beard as none other than Thorn's right-hand man, Ransom. Ransom narrowed his eyes at Wayland, as if trying to figure out why he looked so familiar. Then he turned back to his cohort and continued to chat.

Wayland was oddly relieved—his anonymity was saved for a few more minutes, by the dim lighting, the beard, or maybe both. He ordered a shot of bourbon and glanced around to see if there were other Tundra shifters. He saw one by the pool table. Besides their arctic Tundra white and gray hair and weirdly glowing blue eyes, he could tell the Tundra in their human form by their stupid hipster jacket logos—a mountain peak with a badly drawn wolf atop it. Its head was way too big for its body and it wore a cartoonish grin. He snorted at this under his breath. Wayland was normally a cynical bastard with a sharp tongue, but lately he was moodier and more sarcastic than even he could stand.

Wayland kicked back the rest of his bourbon, strode over to Ransom and tapped him on the shoulder. Ransom spun around. "Hey, man, want to play a game of pool? You look like a guy who's a straight shooter," Wayland wisecracked.

Ransom frowned like he couldn't be bothered. But he must considered, because he excused himself from his buddy and nodded his assent.

conversation went from cordial to tense while they ol.

"Has Ice Lake changed over the years?" Wayland asked, shooting a ball into the pocket.

Ransom shrugged. "Sure. More lodges crowding us out. Par for the course, I suppose." He took a shot and the ball landed just short of the pocket. He grunted.

"You still like it? I mean, are you a lake swimmer or a hiker or…?" Wayland's shot landed near Ransom's ball.

"Why?" Ransom chalked his pool stick. "Did you ever live here?" He narrowed his crystal blue eyes at Wayland. "You sure ask a lot of questions. His shot had an awkward spin to it, and he sank his own ball but not Wayland's. "Shit!" he grumbled.

"Yeah, I've spent time at Ice Lake." Wayland's blood boiled. His inner werewolf was itching to fight.

Ransom leaned against his pool stick and studied Wayland. "Hey, I know you. It was the beard that threw me off. You're motherfucking Wayland Leblanc, aren't you?"

"The last Leblanc standing, due to your greedy tin pot dictator." Wayland could feel his eyes grow hot as his supernatural visioning clicked into place. He saw inside Ransom to his elevated pulse and his roiling gut, revealing his fear of retaliation. "And this time, it won't be me that goes down," Wayland warned.

The two shifters raised their pool sticks and began to spar. Wayland's muscles swelled and his claws sprang out, transforming him into a snarling werewolf. Ransom also shifted, to a shrewd, steroidal beast with wild white fur and a sneering maw.

The few men in the bar moved back to give the shifters space. It was against the rules of shifter engagement to pile on without invitation. Besides, it was free entertainment.

Wayland shoved Ransom into the barstools, which fell in a clattering line.

Distracted by a pretty, dark-haired woman who called

out in objection, Wayland lost focus long enough for Ransom to jab his pool stick into Wayland's ribs. The thing punctured Wayland's flesh before it cracked in half. Wayland went down, thinking his rib was surely broken.

"Take it outside!" yelled the bartender when a table overturned, and growls and shouts exploded like fireworks throughout the beer-laden room.

Wayland pulled the broken stick out with a howl. He and Ransom wrestled their way through the front door and continued the desperate struggle in the weedy grass in front of World's Edge. A small crowd of Tundras and other curious onlookers stood by, most cheering for Ransom, though one or two were drunk enough to cheer for both sides. Ransom landed vicious slashes to Wayland's arms and chest, the areas not protected by Wayland's now raggedy vest. Wayland, in turn, gripped hanks of Ransom's hair and pulled them clear out of the scalp, causing Ransom to yowl in agony. The fight moved behind the club, and the two alphas continued to tangle near the cliff's edge where others had lost their lives in similar fights.

Despite Wayland's throbbing rib, he used his larger size to his advantage. Leaping onto Ransom's curved back, Wayland clamped with his claws and bit deeply into Ransom's neck, back, and already raw scalp with his slavering fangs. Ransom yowled in anguish.

But the beautiful brunette yelling and pumping her fists was a complete distraction, and the next thing Wayland knew, Ransom had managed to twist around, take the upper hand, and deliver a stunning blow to Wayland's head.

Wayland staggered, dizzy, toward the tree line as he saw Ransom fall from his side eye. Every inch of him screamed in searing pain. He stumbled into the forest and fell face down on a pungent bed of pine needles.

* * *

HE STARTLED AWAKE, only able to open one eye. The other was swollen shut. Looking at his arms and legs, he realized he was back in human form, splattered with blood, and on his back in a pine forest. When he tried to lift his head higher, it throbbed mercilessly. His broken rib burned.

There was something, or *someone*, rustling around near him. Was it Ransom, ready to deliver the fatal blow? Eliminate the last Leblanc from the face of the earth?

Holy crap! I'm not ready to die.

Wayland was able to focus with his good eye. It was the woman he saw at the bar. She looked so familiar. Where had he seen her? A sense of déjà vu told him he'd known her for many years, but he still couldn't place her. Up close, she was breathtaking with long raven hair, full lips, creamy skin, and blue crystalline eyes.

Arctic eyes! From the Tundra pack!

Wayland jerked upright to run but fell, groaning in agony.

"Shhh. Don't move," said the woman, kneeling by him.

"Who are you?" Could it be his old Tundra playmate, Stormy? They hadn't seen each other for years. It was rumored that Thorn had kept her so protected it was like she was locked in an ivory tower prison. Holy damn. If it was Stormy, he should have nothing to do with her. She was Thorn's little sister. Could he still be confused? He'd just been hit so hard that maybe his brain had gone haywire. "Where's Ransom?"

"He's alive, but you messed him up good. Why are you coming around, so angry, gunning for a fight? You look so familiar, but…"

She ran a cooling cloth over Wayland's swollen eye. She smelled of forest phlox and river moss—of the Canadian tundra in summer. He struggled again to get up and realized she'd tied him down by his arms, torso and ankles with thick vines. He didn't believe in hurting a woman, but his rage bubbled dangerously close to the surface. If he stayed like this much longer, and she leaned closer to him while cleaning his wounds, he might not be able to stop from snapping his head up and biting her.

"Why the hell did you tie me up?" he snarled.

"For your own safety and for mine. You seemed unhinged. Who are you anyway? You look so familiar."

"Wayland. I used to live around here."

"Wayland!" She stopped cleaning his swollen eye and stared down at him. "Wayland Leblanc."

"Yeah, a damn Leblanc. The Tundras, led by your vicious brother, slaughtered us a year ago, in case you need reminding. Bunch of fucking savages," he growled.

"I know who you are. Your father killed my father."

"So, you *are* Stormy, Thorn's sister," he muttered. *The very man I'm hunting down.*

"Yeah, I'm Stormy. So what?" She threw down the cloth. Her long black hair cascaded forward.

"Your father was only one death," he said bitterly. "Your pack killed my entire family, including my mate and unborn heir."

"Your heir?" A trace of sadness showed in her crystal blue eyes. The memory of Stormy and him wrestling together as little cubs wafted in.

His own unborn would never get to play with other cubs, and never get to glimpse Ice Lake or the regal Canadian woodlands. "That's right, my unborn daughter. Sabine, rest her soul, was going to have our little girl. That's what her note said…but neither lived." Wayland's voice cracked.

"I'm sorry," Stormy murmured. "Life is cruel sometimes."

"The Tundras are beyond cruel. They're sadistic!" he

shouted. "I hate you. I hate your murderous, mad Tundra pack. Untie me or I'll bite my way out of these flimsy bonds."

"Why have you come back?"

"To right the wrongs," he snarled. *For pure revenge.*

"Then I'll never untie you. I'll sink my fangs into your jugular right now. Sever it. Put the last of the Leblanc Royal Wolf line out of his own damn misery." She leaned over and sniffed his neck. In doing so, she turned to wolf herself— elegant, with an inquisitive nose and bright eyes. She was hesitating, like him. He wondered why she didn't sink her fangs into him right then. He hated to admit she was as beautiful in this form as she was in her human form. She had soft white fur and delicate gray markings around her eyes, almost like manicured brows, which moved with her changing expressions. Her moss and phlox scent had grown muskier. He was aroused despite his loathing. With his special vision, he saw her blood seethe with a vicious hatred, mixed with traces of desire and thirst. When she snarled back, her ivory fangs were strangely sexy.

Wayland was torn in a million directions. But he'd had enough. And if he stayed any longer, he wouldn't just bite her, he might tear her from limb to limb. Despite his screeching pain, he roused his full werewolf strength, bolted upright, snapped the bindings open with a loud popping sound, and bolted into the forest, scenting the way back to his camp.

CHAPTER 2

$\mathcal{S}$tormy

HE'S BACK. The one she was obsessed with as a girl cub. The one who nipped her ears when they played together on Ice Lake. The one from the rival pack, which was brutally slaughtered at her brother, Thorn's behest. The only Leblanc to escape the murders was Wayland. She'd heard through the grapevine he'd fled to Louisiana, though she'd lost touch with him sometime between her teens and adulthood when the pack divisions became stricter. She carried the guilt and horror always, of what her own blood had done to the Leblancs.

She'd thought the man looked familiar when he started the fight at World's Edge. He was even more familiar when he shifted to wolfish form, all sleek black except for his eyes that glittered green then gold. Did he recognize her from the start? The way he stared at her. How he didn't look away, even though it cost him the fight with Ransom, Thorn's ride or die.

She couldn't keep herself from tending his wounds. His body was exquisite, molded in hard muscle and quicksilver tendon. At least he had stumbled to the forest edge before he'd fallen. At least they had cover. When he shook off his stupor and said his name, Wayland, hearing him speak it out loud, she was sure of who he was. Her heart exploded in a hundred hot embers. Wayland had been her childhood crush.

But he was also Thorn's most bitter rival. Wayland came here to wreak his revenge.

So, an enemy.

* * *

STORMY SCURRIED into the Tundra's new underground den behind Snow Mountain. It was five miles through the forest from their old den on Ice Lake, and too close to the trendy new Snow Mountain Lodge. Damn, the whole of Canada would soon be one giant tourist lodge if the humans weren't pushed back instead of the wolves. At least the wolf shifters could pose as humans. Rent the lodge rooms and vogue around in trendy ski gear. Keep an occasional eye on the human tourists. Scare them away when the need arose.

"Where are you, Stormy?" Thorn's growling bass was only slightly muffled by the den's dirt walls. "Where the hell did you go?"

"In here, trying to nap," she called from her bed of blue phlox. She nuzzled deeper into the flowers, never tiring of their honeyed aroma.

"Wake up, sister!" Thorn demanded.

"Don't be rude," she griped, already suspecting why he was in turmoil. "Can't it wait?"

"No!" He barged in and gave her a shake. "You saw him, I know you did. Ransom told me everything!" He shook her again, and this time she batted his hands away and sat up.

"Well, if Ransom told you everything, what do you need me for?"

"Don't provoke me. I'm trying to protect us. I thought that royal piece of shit turned tail and ran down to the USA for good." Thorn stuck his hands in his belt where his knives also rested. He stared her down. Even in human form his brows were heavy and more Neanderthal than arctic wolf. It was his temper she hated most. Once he worked himself into a state, he had real trouble calming down, no matter how trivial the reason.

In this case, the reason is not trivial. The reality scared and exhausted her. She played dumb. "What royal piece of shit?"

"Ransom said Wayland Leblanc is back. The royal ass roughed up my second in command. That won't do, not at all. Word is you were talking to Leblanc. Is this true?" Thorn lurched forward. "Don't lie to me!"

"Geez, calm down. He played a game of pool at World's Edge is all, so yeah, I saw the guy." She sighed wearily.

"Ransom said you went off in the woods and spoke to the jerk after he went down."

"Ransom is a damn snoop."

Thorn punched the wall. "How dare you!" Dirt broke away and fell in dusty red clumps. "Ransom is part of *our* royal pack, you ungrateful creature. Everything is our business when we're trying to keep our tribe safe. We're keeping you safe too. Or did you forget that?" His eyes narrowed. "Hey! I'm talking!" He punched the wall again.

"Okay, okay." Stormy doubted her brother was aware of her childhood crush on Wayland. Growing up, she kept her interests close to the vest. Plus, her brother ran with a rougher crew that hunted for squirrels and wood mice, torturing them with glee. No matter that many Tundra had turned into werewolves—from bites wrought in conflicts— and so were more bloodthirsty than regular wolf shifters. According to her, torture for fun was still a sin of nature. But boy cub bullies were often deemed royal warriors in training. And, she had to admit, Thorn had majestically aced his knife skills by the time he was a teen—something to be legitimately proud of. "So, yeah," she replied, "we exchanged a few words. What's that phrase? Keep your friends close and your enemies—"

"Closer." Thorn had calmed down enough to chuckle at this.

She brainstormed like crazy in the span of seconds. She was already determined to talk to Wayland more, and needed a way to cover her plans to follow the uncanny instinct she was gifted with: an ability to track folks, to fly in spirit to places when the moon was high, and to sense things even foreign to wolves. To send her voice out in space, talk *through* people, wolves, and even fish in the creeks. "Yeah, so I'll be your eyes and ears, brother. I'll keep tabs on the guy."

"What's in it for you?" His tone seeped with suspicion.

"Like you say, protection."

Or connection, or temporary protection for Wayland until I know more. Or just...

She didn't even know. All she knew was there was so much energy between her and Wayland it could set the forest on fire.

"Okay. Report back to me. If that fucker thinks he's going to go to war against the Tundra..." Thorn snickered. "It'll be one lone wolf against a whole damn militia of werewolves. We'll mess that guy up so bad that he'll be begging to be booted to hell where his whole damn pack went. Slow torture. He'd get off too easy with a fast kill."

Stormy cringed, but made a show of nodding. Thorn and

the Tundra had provided her comfortable shelter, ample food, and loyal family. It was only right to return the loyalty. Wayland was just a childhood fascination. She was pretty sure which side she was on. But it couldn't hurt to do some detective work.

CHAPTER 3

$\mathcal{W}$ayland

FOR THE FIRST time since before Sabine's murder, Wayland slept like the dead without the aid of sleeping pills. When he woke up in the morning, he heard the sound of animated conversation from the next camp over.

"What's all the jabbering?" he muttered.

At least he could open both eyes, courtesy of whatever weird salve the devious she-wolf Stormy applied. Peering through the trees, he spotted a silver camper with two folding chairs and a line of decorative black ravens and purple owls stuck in the ground. A stylish twist to the typical boring pink flamingoes—he'd give them that.

The neighboring camper had a companion. They were chanting over a glass ball circled by herbs. With his special visioning, he stared at them and sensed their witch essences —tiny familiars perched on each of their shoulders.

The blonde woman had a bust that was practically

pouring from her tank top. Her familiar was a red salamander. The other was tall and dark-haired with breasts like two small apples. Her familiar was a huge moth with wings like black lace.

He liked witches. Hell, DeSoto Parish was full of them. They could give a fantastic reading that offered a sun card, a glimmer of hope to lighten his dark days. Old Nola Jaye was a perfect example. He'd even taken a trip to the Voodoo Museum in New Orleans to get his cards read by a professional when he needed to see which way a Royal Alpha Club battle would go. But here, in the next campsite over?

Damn. I can never get away from women who tempt me, even when I drive to the edge of the known universe. It gave him a sharp pang for his dead mate, Sabine, and a sudden burning curiosity about what his unborn infant girl might've looked like. No doubt she would've been a furry live wire, searching out insects, mice, and trouble. He wiped his moist eyes and grunted. He knew he needed to move on, to put his past fully behind him and find another mate. He wasn't ready, bet or no bet. He would do all that after he got his revenge.

Wayland had a hard time hunting for food. When he tried to stalk prey, his ribs still ached, though Stormy's salve on his chest and belly had closed the puncture wounds from the pool stick and the Tundra wolf's claws. That and a werewolf's sped up healing.

After his escape from Stormy's bindings, he saw she'd already removed his torn shirt and flung it over a log. "You got a good look at my six-pack, eh?" he mumbled at the memory. "Did it turn you on?"

The trek through the northern pine air helped clear Wayland's head and raised his spirits. Eventually he snatched two fat hares, a weasel and a badger. Heading back to the camp, he sensed someone or something following him.

Turning slowly, he spied a few scruffy, skinny coyotes, obviously tracking him because of the fresh kill.

Sometimes coyotes attacked wolves. Other times they waited and fed off the wolves' discards. He stared deeply into their wily amber eyes and saw desperation there. One was poised to attack.

"No need for that. No need! Here you go." Wayland tossed them the fattest hare. They whooped and fought over it. "Hey, share and share alike!" Wayland warned as they snarled over their meager meal. He slunk off before they demanded more of his haul. Down south, he'd suffered coyote bites that got infected. Their bites were nasty and sometimes rabid. Those scrappy bastards were no joke, he thought with grudging admiration.

When he was a distance from the coyotes, he tore into the badger to satisfy his own hunger. Back at camp, he took care to fire up the grill for the remaining hare to make a show of being human. Did the women see through his ruse like he saw through theirs?

* * *

LATER THAT AFTERNOON, Wayland prowled around the old Tundra Den in an attempt to locate his archenemy, Thorn, and catch him unaware. The abandoned den was two miles from the World's Edge bar, in dense woods near Ice Lake. The Leblanc Pack had always been wary of the Tundra's headquarters, and vice versa. The Leblanc's old sanctum, on the other side of Ice Lake, had been decimated when the pack was slaughtered and reverted to pine and bramble. Wayland was painfully aware the spilled blood of the Leblancs had fertilized many trees in this area. The thought made him heartsick.

Supposedly, the Leblanc pack had provoked the war by

infringing on the Tundra turf. It was true that even up here in the Canadian wilderness, encroaching towns pinched the wolves' hunting grounds. But Wayland knew what really sparked the war was Stormy's dad's wandering eye and his crude attempt to steal Wayland's dad's mate. Stealing away a fated mate was a crime in any royal pack.

After peering through the bushes, staking out the site for a good forty minutes, Wayland realized the den was abandoned. He stayed in his wolfish form to scuttle into the den and inhaled deeply, checking for live scents before he padded into each side tunnel and burrow. One lair had a soft bed of pale blue forest phlox, still beautiful even though it had long since dried.

Stormy's old room. The realization came with a flood of unwanted desire.

Each room was empty of wolves and their possessions, even the grand space in the center where packs held council meetings.

Damn.

He realized the Tundra must have built a new sanctuary elsewhere.

Is it because they figured I might return to avenge my royal bloodline?

In his frustration, Wayland tore down the only thing left —herbs hanging from the ceiling, which they had left to dry. He crushed them underfoot and then went farther, kicking up packed dirt—anything to release his pent-up frustration. In his mad scrambling, he unearthed something with a hard corner. A storage box was under the floor, and in it was a trail map! He thrust the leather map under his belt and exited the den. He wore a whip as a belt even when he was in full alpha wolf form, because he never knew when he might need to use it to stash something like the map...or to use the whip for tickling in play or cracking hard in war.

While he chuckled over this, he felt a sudden breeze on his back, and a stink of Tundra. He spun around. A trio of fierce arctic wolves abruptly surrounded him. He cursed himself for being so off his game to be taken unawares. "Where's Thorn?" he growled, noticing Ransom was not in this number. They were third and fourth tiered shifters.

"None of your business," the biggest one rumbled.

"You've come way too late," said another with a snicker.

His internal visioning scanned them. In their sparkling eyes he detected a desire to kill, but also fear and resentful admiration! "Ha!" Wayland snarled, "I see you still respect the Leblancs, you shitheads!"

"We ran your kind out and we'll do it again!" roared the biggest wolf.

Wayland didn't flinch even though he wondered what supernatural advantage these alphas might have. The hard snap of his jaw brought blood to the wolf blocking his path. He slid around the shifter and dashed outside. Another wolf leapt on him and attempted to sink a fatal bite, but Wayland twisted, and the wolf's fangs sliced his right shoulder flank. Blood spurted in time to Wayland's rapid heartbeat. No time to falter, though. Wayland dug his pincer-like claws into the wolf's neck and slammed him, hard, against a tree. Two down. The third wolf jumped on him but couldn't quite latch on. Wayland, grunting from the effort, shifted to human so he could grab the wolf's tail and twirl him. With every frenzied spin, Wayland smashed the wolf against a boulder. He reveled in the sound of the wolf's tortured howls. Finally, he tossed the disfigured wolf behind the boulder and stalked off. These bastards would pay, and pay again, for their cruel killing of the Leblanc dynasty.

This time Wayland had fought well. He badly maimed all three Tundra shifters, while he suffered only one gory flank wound. He wrapped the gash with wide burdock leaves and pushed off to the campsite. High off his revenge binge, he was in good enough spirits to accept an invitation to join the neighboring camp ladies for dinner. Back in human form, he even scrubbed off in the creek, donned a decent shirt and jeans, and brought over freshly caught fish.

While he helped grill the fish, the women asked him a bunch of intrusive questions. He tried to keep his answers vague.

"Where are you from?"

"Louisiana."

"Oh, my! You drove up here from New Orleans?"

"Well, north of that city. Up in western Louisiana."

"I'd love to go to Mardi Gras sometime!" she rushed on. "Growing up in New England, as I did, a Northern gal could really enjoy the Southern sunshine." The blonde woman, Suze, shamelessly flirted, and he considered bedding her just because he could.

"How about you?" Wayland turned to the brunette, Jacey. "Are you from around here?"

"Not really."

What did that even mean? His eyes stayed on her and worked to peer inside her head. Though he had perceptive visioning skills, she was adept at putting up a spooky wall. All he saw was her invisible black moth, fluttering madly about her head. Freaking witches.

Jacey asked him how he spent his afternoon.

"Exploring the woods around Ice Lake," he answered as he stared into the campfire.

"Nice area," she answered, "but dangerous. It's filled with wolf packs and coyotes. God forbid you run into a rabid one." She visibly shuddered.

"How do the arctic wolves get along with the coyotes?" he asked.

"Not well!" She shook her head. "The coyotes can't get

enough food now. The arctic wolves are running them out of the best hiding places."

"I bet those coyotes are hopping mad," ventured Wayland, a plan slowly welling up.

"Yeah, I hear it's just one pack after the other being run out," added Jacey, who seemed to know more than Suze.

"Yeah, well...rabies," he muttered. "Wouldn't want to get on the wrong side of a coyote."

"Rabies is no joke," Suze agreed.

"We've all gotta avoid bites." He managed a wink.

"Bite me anytime," Suze cooed as she loaded the plates with fish and rice. Wayland's thoughts drifted to when he saw the bed of phlox in Stormy's empty Tundra den and then to the image of her snarling over him.

The trio laughed at Suze's wisecrack and dug into their dinner.

Despite his initial reservation, Wayland allowed himself to get drunk. Before he knew it, he was dancing with Suze and then Jacey. Then all three locked arms and did a drunken jig to some cockamamie elfish folk rock the ladies had on their playlist. He ended up liking Jacey because she was subtler and slinky in her touch. He never liked the grabby women best—their lust was too front and forward. Sure, tits in face eventually. But not until the slow burn—the heat turned up in sexy increments so he got used to it and it didn't scorch him.

After dozens of jigs and swigs of hard liquor, the ladies broke out a bag of jumbo chocolate bars and marshmallows and they roasted s'mores.

Wayland found himself skunk drunk, in Jacey's arms. Suze grumbled, but seemed resigned to her friend getting the guy. Jacey smelled slightly like river moss, too, but Wayland figured most campers around here did, because they probably washed their clothes in the rivers and creeks.

Later, still in his blackout, he recalled moments, blips: her earnest kisses and perky tits in his mouth, and how her hips swiveled in waves, one right after the other. His dick hardened, ruled by its own anarchy.

He crawled out of her tiny room in the back of the ladies' RV in the middle of the night and passed out in his own. His dreams weren't of Jacey at all, but of Stormy and her crystalline eyes, her mesmerizing scent, her gentle touch soothing his swollen eye.

"What the actual fuck!" he muttered to himself when he was half awake. He needed to shake off the disturbing fixations because for chrissakes, Stormy was a Tundra wolf, and he came to murder her brother!

Fully awakened by frantic screams countered by fierce roars, he scrambled out of his camper to find a gigantic grizzly rampaging the women's camp. Clearly, it was attracted by all the chocolate and marshmallows wrappers scattered over the site. The bear was on its hind legs, and shaking the camper with its massive mitts. With another roar, it stuck its snout through their camper door.

"Shit!" yelled Suze, throwing a pot of water at it.

"Don't! You'll make it angrier!" shouted Jacey.

Transforming in nanoseconds to fur, fangs, claws, and slavering, snapping jaws, Wayland attacked in full werewolf mode, imbued with a supernatural strength. He and the bear wrestled, rolling around in the dirt. The bear's weight on Wayland crushed his lungs, and the bear's yellowed teeth were like sharpened pole axes. Yet Wayland delivered a melee of deadly fang bites on the bear's torso, and all down his powerful arms.

With each new grinding bite, the bear roared in pain. Even though Wayland's flank wound burst open and the bear slashed his back with dreadful claws, Wayland prevailed. Still in the bear's grip, but with an arm freed, Wayland killed the beast with a deep crosswise slash to its neck, uttering a blood-curdling howl.

The women emerged in their underwear and stared at Wayland's wolfish form. Suze seemed utterly shocked and terrified, and scuttled back inside. She called to Jacey. "Stop! Don't come out! The bear's dead but there's a wild wolf out here!"

Jacey stared with something like ancestral recognition. Or was that Wayland's overstressed, overactive brain conjuring bullshit?

CHAPTER 4

S tormy

OH, blessed goddess of night! The moon helped Stormy's troubled spirit soar through the cooling clouds. She hovered first above his minicamper, then floated next door, above the flickering fire, and saw it all. Wayland was camping next to two women, and he had joined them at their picnic table. She saw the black moth and red salamanders surrounding the auras of each woman—witches and their familiars. She'd always liked witches and fortunetellers, though her brother scoffed at them, and called them halfbreeds and vulgar cons.

The heck with Thorn and his purity tests.

This was Stormy's chance to embody one! She could likely gain access to Wayland through one of them. The idea of it made her heart race. She chose Jacey—she was more simpatico with her own aura.

The dancing, the fiddle music, and the heat of the fire all made Stormy giddy. And, oh, the pleasure of Wayland's hard body pressed up against her was a sweet, forbidden thrill. *All possible through Jacey.* It was a celestial underhanded, sensual joy. Her old crush was sliding and grinding on her.

Wayland took her by the hand, and they fell together onto Jacey's bed. *Oh, the openmouthed, passionate kiss!* The feel of his hands all over her breasts.

Unexpected jealousy rolled through her like creek water spoiled by runoff from weed killer. *It's me, but not really me because he doesn't know it.* The exquisite sensuality of his warm touch she could only steal through Jacey.

That was...until she realized Wayland's head and heart weren't in on the act. He was in a blackout—his head was thick with booze and his dick had an automatic life of its own.

Somehow, this is a relief, however small.

She reminded herself she was only supposed to eavesdrop, and report back to Thorn. But she would never report the sensations she was feeling.

Not to Thorn. Not to Wayland.

She floated in a painful netherworld of isolation, a strange penitence for sleeping with the enemy.

Wayland's killing of the bear was impressive, as was his impulse to protect. The howls, the deep, complete conviction in the fatal bite and slash, the massive creature's brute strength leaving its body and leaking into the midnight sky, into the moon's pale light were all stunning as they played out.

Her deep stare through Jacey's eyes probably gave her away a little, though Wayland didn't know what to look for and didn't yet know what, exactly, he was feeling. His eyes seemed to recognize Stormy was inside Jacey, if only for a fleeting moment. It was so, so hard for her to break away and fly back. She was still obsessed.

CHAPTER 5

 ayland

WAYLAND'S FLANK WAS HEALING, but his ribs still throbbed if he moved too fast. No way he was ready for prime-time battle with the Tundra when he impulsively decided to return to the World's Edge bar. He'd crashed from the recent revenge high and wanted more—needed more, like an addict. The hate broiling in his head and the heaviness weighing on his chest at the slaughter of his entire Leblanc family never let up, even in sleep.

He needed answers to where the Tundra headquarters was, regardless of the danger in going to their bar after the previous brawl. No doubt Thorn knew of his return, and the reason why. But Wayland's careful visioning told him only a couple of Tundra members lurked nearby. He rolled his head back on his muscular neck and breathed in the scents of beer, male sweat, and floor cleanser. His pulse bumped when he smelled phlox. Stormy! He also smelled Tundra blood, much farther off.

He took the barstool next to Stormy and ordered a rye whiskey. Knocked it down and ordered another. She looked good in her shorts with her tanned legs.

Stormy glanced over with raised brows. "I told you not to come back here."

"I told you I had unfinished business."

"Well, get on with it then. Leave me out of it." She flipped her long hair over a shoulder and sipped her drink.

"Where did the Tundra run off to? I went over there. The place is abandoned." He gave her a long look.

"I could have told you that." A hint of a smile played on Stormy's lips. "Did you find anything interesting in your trespassing?"

He thought of the hidden trail map but held back. "Nice bed of phlox you had. I knew it was your little den, off to the right in the tunnel."

"Forest phlox is my signature."

He leaned her way. "It does have a unique floral scent."

"Careful," she whispered. "The pack. They have keen hearing. There are a couple members nearby, and more coming in a bit."

He shrugged. "Well, then, want to take a walk? Chat about the good old times when cubs from all the packs—Leblancs, Tundras, and Windrunners, hell, even a few snaggle-toothed coyotes—roughhoused together on the shores of Ice Lake?"

Her eyes softened, as if the memories of those young times were still vivid. But, she stayed silent.

"I promise, nothing...below the belt." He chuckled, and then under his breath, he added, "Look, I know we're surrounded by my mortal enemies. I smell them from a mile away. They're dying to attack. But I could just saunter out of here. Meet you on the old Leblanc side of Ice Lake. For nostalgia's sake." Stormy gave an almost undetectable nod. With that, Wayland slid off the barstool and padded out fast.

* * *

If she's coming to Ice Lake, she's sure taking her sweet time.

Wayland was discouraged and irritable. He knew he was playing with fire, and it would only enrage his enemies even more. He had no true answer. Only questions.

Why was he letting himself be distracted by this woman? He only came up here for one thing: to murder her entire pack. Where was Thorn? Ransom? Why hadn't they attacked him at the World's Edge earlier today? A worrying thought came to him. What if they'd decided to rough up their pack sister instead of him in some twisted form of punishment for both him and Stormy?

There was a loud rustle in the brambles. *It's her!* His irritation dissolved into relief. She had changed from shorts into jeans, hiking boots and a tight black T-shirt with *Untamed* emblazoned across her full chest. He tried not to stare but didn't succeed. Stormy was a regal queen, even with her raven hair swept up in a sensible ponytail.

She approached him and sat, cross-legged. "Okay, you got me here. What's on your mind? I mean, before you go and kill my pack." She let out a scornful guff of air.

"Why are you so devoted to a bunch of bloodthirsty killers?" he asked.

She shrugged. "Us wolves, we're all killers, especially the ones who get turned. It's life—the law of the wild. What makes you so high and mighty? Besides, aren't we going to reminisce about playschool on Ice Lake? The rough and tumble of furry wolf cubs all splashing together in the water, wrestling in the bramble?" She laughed. "You *were* a cute little critter. I remember your sleek black markings, the way you liked to bite my ears."

He snorted. "The equivalent of pulling your braids. You used to corner me in the bramble." His voice grew husky. "Your markings are still cute when you turn wolfish. The delicate black lines around your eyes."

"If I weren't so sure we were enemies, I'd say you were flirting with me, Mr. Leblanc."

He raised a quizzical brow. "Tell me, why did the Tundra change headquarters?"

"They needed a bigger space. The pack grew in size."

"After it decimated its rivals," he spit out. "Where are the new digs?"

"Ah, ah, ah! Not so fast." She narrowed her eyes at him. "Why would I blow the locale? Decimation of territorial rivals is the law of the jungle."

Wayland frowned. "Really? The packs all tolerated each other for quite a while."

"Until the food source grew scarce. Until the forests got swallowed by the suburbs."

"Until your father tried to steal my father's mate right under his nose."

"Don't make this petty, Wayland."

"Just keeping it real. Besides, suburban spread wasn't the fault of the Leblanc pack. And was it also the law of the jungle to kill the *females* of our pack?"

Stormy sighed. "She-wolves make babies…that grow into dangerous adult male enemies." Her expression darkened. "I'm sorry you lost your heir. I really am."

"My unborn child was a girl."

"Oh. That's sad." Stormy's eyes glazed over. "Look, I don't make the rules."

"I'm a damn alpha and even alphas don't always make the rules," Wayland grumbled. "How's this for a crappy rule from the head of the royal shifters? They said since the royal wolf dynasties are being killed off and fading to nothing, we all have to go out and breed, produce an heir within the year, or be booted from the club and lose our royals status. How do you like that shit?" His laughter was bitter.

"Quite mercenary."

"You ain't heard nothin' yet," Wayland replied. "One of the Louisiana royals connived me into betting money on who could be the first to impregnate a she-wolf. What a crap way to find a mate, much less a *fated* mate." He shook his head in disgust. "I mean, I like sex, but for chrissakes, give me a break."

Stormy threw her head back and howled in laughter. "So, am I the intended receptacle?"

"Now *that* would be a soap opera for the ages. We'd be Romeo and Juliet and we'd both be killed by pissed off family rivals in the final act."

"Makes for a good melodrama," she quipped, taking her hair out of its clip to let it fall loose around her shoulders. "What would they call that on Broadway? The name 'Romeo and Juliet' is already taken. I know, War for Love!"

"Murder at Ice Lake," he replied.

"The Massacre of Fated-Mates."

"Losing Hearts and Minds," he said.

"Love, Death, and S'mores," she added.

Wayland and Stormy fell backward, giggling. Stormy's hair cascaded through the underbrush. Wayland reached over to help her untangle it, and their hands touched. He leaned in and took the sudden liberty of kissing her on the cheek—a chaste kiss, or so he thought. "Just for old cub times," he whispered, "like nipping your ears."

"Or cornering you in the bramble," she said breathlessly and kissed him on the mouth.

They heard a loud rustling and froze, both assuming the

worst. Flashes of fiery fur whizzed past them, followed by smaller blurs. "Foxes and their kits," Wayland said. "We've scared them out of their den."

Stormy pulled back. "This won't work. Not even in jest. My brother will kill you."

Wayland pulled back, too. "One of us will kill the other. That seems fated. But I shouldn't put you in harm's way. I'm sorry." He stood and offered her his hand.

She rose on her own. "I'll see my way out of here." With that, she was gone.

Wayland was crushed yet strangely buoyed at the same time. She kissed him. He didn't dream it. The press of her lips on his still vibrated. He lifted his hand to his mouth and held it there, going over their conversation. The play titles they'd invented were hilarious. So, Stormy was witty on top of being beautiful. Though that last title she'd thought of was an odd coincidence. What had made her use the word s'mores?

Maybe there was a way to wreak his revenge on Thorn yet lure Stormy to his own side, unharmed. Break her loyalty to her brother, her pack.

Impossible.

But what if it isn't?

What if he could uncover an action Thorn took that was so horrendous, so cruel…that Stormy might be led to switch allegiances? Thorn's father was a philandering piece of shit, and they said the fruit didn't fall far from the tree. In the meantime, Wayland needed to build up an army—one approximating the Tundra's numbers if he was going to have a fighting chance. But how?

* * *

BACK AT THE CAMP, the ladies next door invited him for another dinner. He wavered, but accepted. It was a distraction from Stormy's off-limits charms. The women had a Tarot deck spread out on the picnic table, surrounded by flickering candles. It was an elemental deck with rather cool animals. After dinner, he asked them to read his cards and Jacey volunteered. He pulled the hermit—probably him—depicted as a fox, alone in a den. And many cards that showed swords.

"Battles," Jacey declared.

Wayland shuddered, recalling Thorn was an expert knife-wielder.

"Choose three more," she suggested. He handed them over, and she turned them as she placed them on the table.

"Wow! All these dogs," he noted. "Dogs holding cups, dogs running with pentacles, a dog braying at the moon. What do you make of it?"

Jacey's dark eyes flashed. "It balances out the hermit and the profusion of knives. It's a better fate—a leg up in battle. Does this mean anything to you?"

Dogs are like coyotes, he realized, nodding slowly. "Yeah, I'm not totally sure but…"

Coyotes!

Suze brought over a new bottle of wine and popped the cork. "Another round, good people?"

Wayland held up his hand. "Not for me, thanks. I'm already buzzed and don't want to get wasted like the other night." He chuckled. "Jacey, interesting reading."

She got up from the table and wound her way around to Wayland. "Wanna cuddle?"

"Sounds like fun," he drawled. They wandered over to the camper.

Woozy and horny, he bedded Jacey. The tall, slinky brunette reminded him of Stormy but wasn't as dangerous, and sleeping with her wasn't a Romeo and Juliet type suicide mission. Although, like before his dick did its thing without his brain being involved. No danger in getting his heart tangled up in Jacey. He was nowhere near ready to commit to a fated mate and breed an heir. He was still in full-tilt rebellion mode. Screw all the know-it-all pack Royal honchos from Louisiana. Though he did miss his alpha buddies, Dorian, Alec and even Tobias. The rules were different up here in his native Canada. At least he could keep pretending for a while more.

* * *

DURING THE NEXT FEW DAYS, he avoided The World's Edge Bar, the old Tundra Den, even Ice Lake. He didn't try to find Stormy, either. But that didn't stop him from thinking about the way her hair felt, sifting through his fingers, or how soft her lips were, pressing on his. He decided to go hunting for food, lots of food, and search out the coyotes. It was a great distraction.

Coyotes were a scruffy bunch, and didn't trust him—either in human or wolf form. These shifters were typically afraid of humans, and wolves weren't their favorite critters, either. They especially shied away from any turf that wolves had pissed on—they detested the stench of it—though they weren't against stealing the rest of any wolf dinner left behind. So, when Wayland was near, they hung back, snarled, and patrolled the perimeter of their den with snapping jaws and loud warning yips.

But the lure of Wayland's fresh kills beckoned—possum, hares, badgers, squirrels, fat fish from the creeks, and even a deer. He kept on delivering, and the coyotes were too hungry to resist for long. They came creeping out, skittish and slit-eyed. He made them pad almost right up to his feet before he dropped the bait. They snapped it up and ran, whipping their heads around suspiciously to make sure he wasn't hunting them.

By day five, he'd gained enough trust to communicate in more ways. He changed to wolf form to speak to them in the language of the wild. He explained he needed to build an army, and that he respected the coyotes as fierce warriors, unafraid to take risks. They asked him who he needed to fight and why. He explained it all. The coyotes were loyal pack beasts, too, and the story of Wayland's mate and unborn child being killed aroused their sympathy and anger. No love was lost between their ranks and the Tundra.

"Just because they come from a royal line, those arctic wolf bastards think they rule Canada," growled Bones, the head coyote. He towered over the others in his pack, and had a distinctive black stripe traveling the length of his tan muzzle.

Red Claw, the coyotes' second in command, with a ruddy coat one could practically see in the dark, agreed. "Yeah, when we come into World's Edge in our human form, Tundra think they rule the bar, hogging the seats and the pool tables. They even flirt with our females, though they would kill every one of us if we flirted with theirs. Royal snobs." He emitted a sharp yip for emphasis.

Wayland, a royal alpha himself, swayed them away from more trash talk about royals. Instead, he stressed how the Tundra would soon steal all the hunting grounds. "They're overbreeding and they're selfish. They care nothing about other packs' rights to the wilderness. They're cruel. Next, they'll be murdering *your* unborn cubs, right in their mamas' bellies." Wayland paused dramatically to let it sink in.

Bones stalked forward and stood muzzle-to-muzzle with Wayland. "As long as you keep the pack in fresh meat so no one goes hungry, we'll side with you."

"Not just side with me. Fight with me," insisted Wayland.

"Fight with you," growled Red Claw, also stepping up. "Spy for you, kill for you."

Bones turned to his pack, spread out in front of their den. "What do you say, coyotes?"

"Fight with you, spy for you, kill for you!!" howled the entire pack.

CHAPTER 6

tormy

I MUST BE MORE CAREFUL! No more blurting out clues like the s'mores, or Wayland will know I floated into his camp.

She wouldn't be able to throw her spirit into Jacey's to enjoy the pressure of Wayland's skin, hot against hers. She wouldn't be able to hear his urgent moans, stolen from Jacey. She saddened, knowing it was the only way she'd ever have him that close, because she was Tundra, and Wayland was a sworn enemy.

That night, she couldn't keep away. She waited until the pack finished their last beers, their final rowdy conversations over the fire. She padded silently past Thorn's den to make sure he was out of it. Yes, he was wheezing, the sloppy snore of the sot. She cringed, remembering him boasting tonight to Ransom about how he'd track Wayland down and twist a knife between his ribs while he was sleeping. Better yet, he'd stab him in broad daylight, so he'd never lay his greedy eyes on Stormy again. Thorn told Ransom that his sister didn't even have to confess her feelings for Wayland. He could see the disgusting truth in her lovelorn eyes.

This frightened Stormy. Her brother was dangerous enough when in a good mood. Get on his bad side, and he was capable of demented things: the capricious slaughter of a human at World's Edge who bumped into him by mistake, setting fire to Stormy's last boyfriend's feet when he caught them by the forest cliff doing things he couldn't unsee, and his childhood glee in torturing small animals.

He had a good side, though. He could be generous. He'd always given her the best room in the pack den, he cooked her favorite dishes, and he'd fought off a bobcat that stalked her at Ice Lake, though that didn't quite compare to Wayland's masterful kill of the intruding bear. Stormy smiled at the memory. But blood was thicker than…what? Was it more essential than a longed-for kiss? A sexy glance from a lifelong crush returning?

Stormy closed her eyes and stretched out on the bed of phlox. She let her spirit soar through the cooling, starry sky. She steered on the breezes until she saw the campfire, and Wayland sitting with the blonde and the tall brunette at the picnic table, reading Tarot.

Stealthily, weightlessly, she sank into Jacey. Jacey was taller and skinnier than Stormy, and cooler in body temperature. It was such a strange feeling, inhabiting another. But Stormy felt the need to warn Wayland, since she knew firsthand the approaching danger.

Stormy, through Jacey, plunked down the ten of swords. It depicted a castle with ten swords stuck in the ground by its moat. An animal of some sort was swimming in the water. "I see you prowling way outside of your territory. A lethal beast tracks you. Use extreme caution." Stormy gazed at Wayland through Jacey's confused self.

"Really?" Suze looked askance at the card, and then over at Jacey. "I see that card more as a protective fortress."

Wayland grimaced as he glanced from one to the other woman over the flickering candlelight. "Well, which is it ladies? Is that a coyote in the water, or what? I am kind of excited about the coyotes. I'm training them to help me fight. Bones is a darn good guy, and Red Claw, his second in command too. In my last reading the cards were full of dogs. That's when I got the idea."

"Fabulous!" Suze gushed. "I'm glad we could help you. Even if it involves those tatty coyotes." She giggled. "Who knows? Maybe they're wily beasts in bed."

"Be serious!" Stormy cried, through Jacey. Her dark eyes gleamed with worry. "The enemy is forming their army, too."

"Pretty odd interpretation," Suze scoffed.

Wayland rose, went to the fire, and prodded the dying embers of wood. In minutes, his mood had gone from cheery to pensive to unsure.

Suze stretched her arms and yawned. "This old witch is turning in, folks. Don't you two go eating any s'mores tonight," she joked.

"Nope. No more bears will dare come to this camp." Jacey got up and wrapped her arms around Wayland from the back. She pressed her face between his powerful shoulder blades. He held her forearms and stroked them. For Stormy, it was like heaven floating through every nerve. She lightly nuzzled his shoulder. "Coming to bed?" she whispered in giddy anticipation.

He lifted his hands from her arms and deftly swung free, turning as he did. He gave her a warm hug, followed by a chilling statement. "I'm heading to my camp tonight. I'm kind of *off*, preoccupied. I've been talking to another woman, Jacey. Have to be honest."

Honest! Were men ever really honest? And why did he

feel the need to confess just a chat with a random female? His was a strange confession for two people who hardly knew each other and were simply hooking up in a summer campsite. Stormy's heart raced at the same time she sensed Jacey's hurt.

So, he wasn't into Jacey! That was a relief. But Stormy would dearly miss the warmth of Wayland's naked flesh and his breath on her upturned face. *So, am I the person who holds his attention? He is a catch! Many women must long to be his.* Blue butterflies that loved to alight on phlox fluttered around Stormy, in a necklace like sapphire. Her butterfly familiars fought Jacey's black moth for the prize of reigning in Wayland's world.

Wayland started to walk to his campsite, but stopped. Slowly, he turned to say goodnight when his eyes fixed on something in the air. He stared, openmouthed. "Butterflies at night?" he whispered.

Oh, goddess of midnight! I must be much more careful with my familiars! But how, when I'm so distracted by my aching heart?

CHAPTER 7

Wayland

WAYLAND STARTED a training regimen with Bones, Red Claw, and their coyotes. He was rather impressed so far. Who knew the crafty critters had such a sophisticated system of yips, howls, squeals, barks, wails, and yelps that rivaled Morse code? Who knew they were Olympic swimmers, and conducted some of their scouting at dawn before most lazy shifters even rolled out of bed?

They could burrow into almost any crappy soil to make a hidey-hole, and they did have a warren of them: around Ice Lake, through pockets of forest, and under rocks and tangled vines. But Wayland and the coyotes needed more insight into the Tundra. Where exactly were their headquarters? What were they planning as a counterattack? What were their unique weaknesses?

Wayland fed them well, with fresh kills of badger, fish, and dozens of hares. He enjoyed the hunt—it limbered him, and helped him scout the area, far and wide. The coyotes were grateful and gave him a gift of berries for snacks and burdock for salves.

Tonight, Wayland had invited the two coyote leaders to his campsite for drinks. For this, they all shifted into human form. After all, there were ladies next door, even if they were quirky witches with RV decorations of ravens and a phalanx of purple candles burning on the picnic table.

Bones looked particularly badass in a western shirt with pearl snaps and pointy cowboy boots with spurs that could, with one kick, stamp spiky patterns in someone's skin. He slicked his raggedy brown hair back with what looked like bear grease. It occurred to Wayland that perhaps Bones was the guy who hauled off the grizzly corpse and made good use of it.

Red Claw was arguably more outrageous. He had a linebacker's physique and long pumpkin-hued hair, which he braided Native American style with crow feathers stuck in. He was wearing a Freddie Kruger T-shirt and black jeans, and his hands and arms were so gigantic they could probably lift a jeep.

Wayland settled them into his cheesy mega-store folding chairs, wondering if the chairs would collapse before the night was through. He ferried over the booze and some shot glasses. "Scotch or bourbon, guys?" he asked.

Red Claw chose bourbon and Bones the scotch. "Returning the favor," said Red Claw, and pulled out a leather-bound flask of his own, plus another huge bottle for Wayland. "Blackberry hooch. Made it myself," he declared proudly. Wayland thanked him, and they tossed back multiple shots before launching into a business meeting.

"Did either of you dig up any useful intel?" Wayland asked. He took a swig of the blackberry hooch. It both burned and sweetened as it gurgled down the pipes. It was kind of like drinking pancake syrup mixed with gasoline, but in a good way.

"Yeah, I got some info," Bones reported. "I've been hanging out incognito at the World's Edge, and man, those Tundra shifters sure like to flap their yappers." He leveled a serious look at Wayland. "They're training a battalion, back between Ice Lake and that ugly new lodge by Snow Mountain."

"Oh, yeah? Snow Mountain Lodge?" Wayland had read about it on Google when he was scouting for places to stay. Camping was an easy choice over that overpriced, oversized log cabin fiasco. "Is that near their den?"

"Not sure yet," Bones admitted.

"Well, find out, okay?" Wayland worked to suppress his irritation, because honestly, he should've figured out where it was himself by now. Bones nodded.

"I'll tell you something else," Red Claw chimed in. "That Thorn dude is working hard to teach his shifters his knife skills." He snorted. "And some of them ain't so talented at it. One clumsy fool dropped the knife straight through his foot." They sniggered at this. Red Claw rubbed his ruddy beard and went on. "Other dudes were quick to learn—real scary shit. Like a boomerang knife throw that lands right between the eyes. And a crazy-mad somersault from behind that got their straw victim a surprise jab to the heart." Wayland and Bones groaned, and Red Claw regarded the two alpha shifters. "What do *we* have? Us coyotes need a special battle skill."

"We could use all of our special hoots," Bones offered, "the secret way we communicate. Total advantage."

"That's the spirit!" Wayland exclaimed. "The Tundra will understand nothing! Plus, what about your expert skill in the water? I read about it online."

Red Claw frowned. "Yeah, but the Tundra pack also have some excellent swimmers."

Wayland shrugged as he rubbed his thumb over his shot glass. "They can still be cornered, though. Even epic swimmers can drown. You can use the element of surprise to your advantage. Yes?"

"Sure, boss." Red Claw nodded, but his red brows were furrowed. "Too bad no guns."

"Absolutely no guns," Wayland affirmed. "Way too loud. It would alert the goddamn human police force and FBI to our shadow world. But…" He brushed a hand through his wavy hair and stood up. "I use a fighting tool that's never let me down, either in human or werewolf form, and I brought extras. Want a demo?"

"We're all eyes," Bones replied.

Wayland unwound the whip from his belt-loops and cracked it hard over one of the extra folding chairs. "Imagine this is a Tundra's neck." The cheapo plastic webbed seat split in two and the parts flopped down. His coyote buddies gaped and whistled through their teeth. Wayland chuckled. "Thankfully, these chairs were on deep discount. So, you want some whips to train with?" He looked over at Red Claw and Bones, both of whom were enthusiastically nodding.

"That's a big hell *yasssss*," quipped Red Claw.

Wayland secured his whip back in the belt-loops, went into his camper, and emerged with two brimming bags of whips.

Bones did a coyote war whoop.

Slowly, Wayland, Red Claw and Bones brainstormed a strategy involving Ice Lake and laying siege to the Tundra by surrounding them. They scratched out maps and drank some more. Strains of bluegrass wafted their way.

"Who's over there?" Bones cocked his head toward the neighboring camp. "We got some eavesdroppers?"

Wayland batted his hand dismissively. "No worry, guys. Just two witches over there, reading Tarot and playing weird music." His brassy laughter encouraged the coyote shifters to follow suit.

"Well, hell, why don't you introduce us?" Red Claw suggested. "Bones has a mate he's been with for about a hundred years. But hey, I'm footloose and fancy free, as they say." The three shifters laughed harder.

They made their way to the ladies' camp. Suze took an instant liking to Red Claw, and vice versa. Wayland noticed how, when they danced, they fit perfectly—her large breasts against the shifter's stomach, Red Claw's arms encircling her short, stocky figure, her head barely reaching his barrel of a diaphragm. Wayland wanted a mate that fit in an unexpected way, yet perfectly. Someday.

Bones parked his long torso at the witches' picnic table and asked for a Tarot reading, which seemed the logical thing since Jacey was shuffling the deck. Wayland sat too. He was awkward and tongue-tied after rejecting her advances the other night, so he was glad to have company. He also figured she was tense too, because his visioning saw her black moth flitting nervously about her shoulders. He offered her a strained smile. She returned it and went back to the cards.

The first nine cards were general enough to not grip Wayland's attention as Jacey and Bones pored over them.

But the final two cards grabbed everyone. "Water," Jacey said, flipping the card Bone pulled. It depicted a dog swimming. "You will have an intense, uncomfortable experience in a body of water." She turned over his last card and gasped softly. "The Death card. Yours, or another one close to you."

"Gawds!" Bones exclaimed, grimacing. "No other interpretation, eh?"

"Perhaps. It could mean a near death experience," she murmured, but sounded unconvinced.

"Talk about a downer," Wayland grumbled, and slapped

Bones congenially on the shoulder. "Hey, bro, hope you don't mind, I'm beat. I'm going to make it an early night."

Suze called from where she was dancing with Red Claw, in front of the RV, strung with tiny blinking lights. "Just because Wayland here is a party pooper doesn't mean we're kicking you guys out!" Red Claw whooped at this. Bones agreed to another drink before returning to his mate at the coyote compound and agreed to carry back the cache of whips.

Wayland rose from the table and glanced at Jacey with a pang of guilt.

She smiled back wistfully. Her moth familiar now sat listlessly on her shoulder. Curious, he didn't see its butterfly companion he had noticed before. He was tempted to ask her about it, but didn't want to stir her hopes up.

As he walked toward the path to his camp, Jacey followed and tapped him on the shoulder. He spun around, unnerved. "Hey," she started, "it's okay, Wayland. I'm not mad." He nodded, at a temporary loss for words. She went on. "You know, those first times we were playing around, I didn't feel quite myself. It was almost like I was acting like someone else." She paused. "I'm usually more conservative. I mean I don't jump into—"

"Look, I'm sorry. I was really drunk. I was acting like an—"

"No." She placed her arm momentarily on his, in a reassuring gesture. "Don't apologize. It's all good." She gazed intently into his eyes. "It was wonderful and fun. But you are meant for someone else. The one with the butterflies."

Butterflies? Wayland's stomach flipped like the butterflies were fluttering inside him. "But how do you...?"

"I'm a witch, remember?" Her laughter was pure relief.

He reached out. "May I?" She nodded. He gave her an

impulsive hug. "Jacey, you're a lovely person. Thanks." With that, he wove through the narrow, weedy path to his RV.

He was drunk—that blackberry hooch was epic. But he wasn't blackout drunk. He had allies in Bones and Red Claw, he had intel they had generously shared with him, he had two cool witch friends nearby. He had a hunch as to who owned those butterfly familiars.

Pushing up through his weighty despair, Wayland sensed a lightness—was it hope?—for the first time in like, forever.

CHAPTER 8

 tormy

IT WAS nighttime and she'd been watching the spectacle from
the sidelines for an hour by torchlight. Her stomach was in a
tight knot and her temples throbbed with a worsening
headache.

Thorn was in the center of the large, circular field
training his shifters. They lined up and tried their hand at the
targets: leather replicas of Leblanc shifters with the telltale
black fur and green eyes, looking way too much like
Wayland; and hastily made straw replicas of the coyotes—
shaggy and wiry, with lengthy muzzles and amber eyes made
of stone. By torchlight, their fake eyes gleamed with discon-
certing vitality.

Yesterday, Thorn had grilled her about why there was
such an abundance of coyotes lurking about in World's Edge.
He wouldn't shut up about it. He insisted she knew. While
yelling about it, he broke a beer mug and her favorite coffee

cup depicting a sprig of blue phlox. He complained she wasn't delivering on her promise to collect information on Wayland. "What good are you? You're in love with that asshole, is that it? If so, you can pack your bags and go. But you won't be purebred royal Tundra anymore. And you can never return. You'll be dead to us. The outside world is a frightening place. If the half-breeds don't get you, the humans will—one or the other and you'll be taken advantage of, or dead."

He had always used this to scare her. He was obsessed with her being purebred, untainted by another breed's impure blood. He insisted it was the most important thing in the world.

She'd thought of leaving the pack before. Truth was, she was terrified of hitting the road, of being on her own and being mistreated even worse than Thorn could ever do. Thorn had painted a nightmare picture of the outside world, where humans would trap you or kill you or do things for their own sick purposes. If they didn't get you, the monstrous roving gangs that lurked in every crime-ridden city would.

Pack loyalty had also been drilled into her head from childhood—even more so after Wayland's father had killed her dad. And her mother? Well, she never knew her, because she was told her mother died when Stormy was only two. She was also told her mom was a royal, with fur the color of fresh snow—untouchable in her Tundra pack perfection. Sometimes, while drifting off to sleep, Stormy imagined her mother, sitting on a crimson throne, wrapped in a delicate silk robe, or eating gooseberries and cream and drinking pale apricot tea by the fire, set with birch logs. Over the years, Stormy elaborated these images with ever more elaborate fairytale depictions.

Reluctantly, she gave Thorn the lowdown on Wayland's

coyote allies after he threatened to damage her hair that had taken years to grow long. "Give me some damn intel," he'd yelled. "If you don't, I won't just cut your pretty hair, I'll *burn* it!" Thorn wasn't stupid, she rationalized, he would find out sooner or later. It was better than squealing about Wayland's more intimate confidences. But it wasn't—not at all.

When had Thorn gotten so abusive? She remembered him being kind to her, cooking her special cakes and brewing teas he concocted from roots he'd gathered. He was a talented chef, and he had always had time to build up her self-esteem, tell her she was a little Tundra queen and he was proud to be her brother. But he was getting so angry, so craven. Maybe he had always been a horror to others, and now he had added her to that mix. She shuddered. The lines had blurred. Her own brother was becoming a terrifying stranger to her.

Now, she rubbed her head and stared in horror at his martial field exercises.

Thwack! A shifter somersaulted, landed on his feet, and his jackknife hit the Leblanc target squarely between the eyes. A way to leap over obstacles and keep your enemy guessing at your next move, Thorn had explained. The Tundra shifters cheered.

Ransom stepped up, revved his powerful arm in a circle and executed an abrupt machete boomerang that landed where a live heart would've beaten in the coyote mannequin. More wild shouts rang out.

Ugh, thought Stormy. This field of shifters reeked with sour alpha sweat and narcissism, normally nothing of concern, but in her present state, a frightening development.

She was worried for Wayland. She knew they couldn't be together. Her blood and his blood would never mix. Still, she didn't want him to perish. If only he could see this. If only he had a leg up so the inevitable battle would be fair. If she stayed here any longer, she'd be sick right on the grass. She waited until her brother's back was turned. Then she rose and wobbled off. Just before dawn she would take her own swift action.

* * *

SHE RACED through the forest in her wolf form with the *shooshing* sound that rain brought. At the edge of his campsite she paused, transformed to human, and listened. Her supernatural hearing detected the two sleeping women next-door through their lilting breaths, and a male who snored with a rasp. Coyote, she determined.

Then, listening to Wayland's slow and steady breathing, she ached. *He's relaxed, but he won't be for long.* Carefully, she stepped over to his minicamper door and unfastened it and entered on feet quiet as kitten paws on a quilt. She gazed down at him, his wavy black hair slipping around his mountainous shoulders and thick, corded neck. She leaned forward and watched the pulse where the carotid artery sat, just under his skin. She breathed in his heady scent of leather, pine, and blackberries. A keen longing ran through her. If only she could inhabit Jacey again so she could feel Wayland press into her.

Sadly, that part had run its last course.

His lids flickered. She inhaled sharply. He startled awake. He opened his eyes wide, and then narrowed them to green slits. He sprang to a sitting position. "Stormy? What the hell?" His eyes seemed to take her in greedily, from the lake blue skirt that hugged her hips to her low-cut tank top. His gaze locked into hers. "What are you doing here?"

"I… I came to give you some information," she said breathlessly. "Thorn is ramping up the Tundra, training them to kill you. He knows about the coyotes."

"What?" Wayland was fully up now, and he swung his legs around to the floor. He brushed hair from his eyes. "How did…?" he started but didn't finish. He must've either figured Thorn had squeezed it out of her or that any crowd of coyotes in World's Edge was too obvious a marker. "Where are they training?" he asked.

"About five miles behind Ice Lake. Not far from that new Snow Mountain Lodge."

"Where's the damn Tundra den?" he growled.

She hesitated, drew a foot over the camper's metal floor. It was nothing he wouldn't find out soon enough, either through the coyotes or by his own sleuthing. He might as well know now. "It's right under that field where they train. Out in the open. Reverse psychology. Don't hide it, just make the thing so obvious that rival shifters are stepping over it without even suspecting."

"Thanks. It didn't kill you to tell me, now did it?"

"No," she murmured.

"Be careful, Stormy. Visiting me isn't so safe. Are you sure no one followed you?"

She laughed. "At dawn? Only the coyotes get up that early. Tundra like their sleep."

"Point taken. Still, you'd best not stay long. And after this, we should probably make sure we don't cross paths for a week or so. God forbid your damn brother knows we talk at all."

"True." Her skin crawled at the mention of Thorn. She was upset enough at the trickle of information he'd already eked out of her.

Wayland stared at her, unsmiling. "Can I ask you a strange question?"

"Sure."

"Do you ever have butterflies around you? Sort of like an aura of butterflies?"

She stiffened. Oh, waning moons! He had figured things out too soon. "What do you mean?" She feigned innocence with a raised brow.

"How did you know I had s'mores the other week?"

She shrugged. "Doesn't everyone have s'mores when they camp out?"

"C'mon, Stormy. Do you take me for a fool?" He raked a hand through his hair, still mussed from sleeping.

"What do you mean, Wayland?" She was tired of playing dumb. But revealing her secret talent could be dangerous in ways she couldn't predict.

"I guess I have to spell it out. Look, the lady next door is a witch. Her name is Jacey. Wanna tell me about your special gift of throwing your spirit into other people?" Stormy's stomach twisted even tighter. He would hate her now. But she disliked lying. Didn't want to pile on lie after lie until the whole world turned to bullshit. She remained silent, though, so he went on. "Jacey said she felt like someone else was inside her. She apologized for coming onto me so hard." He snickered. "She said she didn't know what got into her, that she was acting like a stranger had taken over her."

"You think that was me? Takes a nerve." Stormy punched him on the shoulder. Her fist came away sore.

"Yeah, I bet it *was* you." Wayland's low growl set Stormy on fire. How did he get to do that? What was she going to say now? She lowered her head and focused on her hands, folded in a sort of prayer pose.

"I see butterflies around you," he said gently. "Jacey said I'd see butterflies, and I do. Hers was a black moth, and for one night the moth was playing with blue butterflies. I was confused, but not anymore." His whisper was like a tender plea. "Stormy?"

She looked up. Big mistake. His eyes were so green, so compelling and so *everything* she had to come clean—*wanted* to come clean. "Yeah, okay, it was me, *in her*. It's a strange talent I discovered I had."

"Indeed," he said wryly. "Can anything interfere with it?"

"Do you want it to?"

He shrugged. "Your…talent…might be inconvenient at times."

"Only metal stops it so far. One time I was in a metal, um, building, and I couldn't do spirit travel. Not until I stepped outside under the moon." Stormy frowned. "Look, I told my brother I would spy on you and… I'm ashamed."

"It was a devious way to get to me, and not so fair to Jacey. What did you see?"

"A man dancing. A man drinking and getting drunk. A man kissing a lady."

"Could you feel my touch when you were inside Jacey?"

"Yes."

"Did you like it?" He leaned closer. His scent of fermented blackberries mixed with pure *need* drove the heat down between her hips, into that dark, mysterious place of carnal feeling.

"I liked it," she admitted. "I wanted more of it. I was jealous of the woman you thought you were kissing." There, she said it. Let him hate her. Let him think she was a freak.

After a moment, where he seemed to be searching an even deeper place in her heart, he wrapped her in his powerful arms and kissed her, openmouthed. She met his tongue and let her head curve back against his arms and rest there, while their tongues explored, their pulses raced, their emotions exploded over each other—messy, hot and desperate for connection.

She didn't stop him when he lowered her to the mattress. She kicked off her boots, curled her fingers through his hair, pulled him closer and kissed him again. He joined in, languidly exploring her teeth, her tongue, and sending waves of exquisite pleasure through her.

"Oh lord, Stormy," he whispered in her ear. "You're so beautiful."

She licked his ear then gave it a firm nip. She loved the sound of his groan. "This is so much better than being with you through the witch," she admitted.

"It is," he whispered.

"I was there when you told her you were talking to another woman. Who was it?" She knew the answer but longed to hear him confess it out loud.

"You. It was you." He kissed her again, stroking her hair and her back, then slid his palms down to her hips.

She moaned and began the first hint of bucking up to meet him through her clothes when a startling clatter on the mini-camper door interrupted them.

"Boss!" Red Claw called out. "You in there?"

"He's my coyote ally," Wayland whispered. "Don't know what he'll think if he sees a Tundra in my bed, but—"

"No way!" Stormy jumped up, straightened her shirt, and threw on her boots.

"Wayland?" The coyote shifter knocked again. "Hey!" he bellowed. "I thought we could grab a bite before training."

Stormy slid through the bathroom window and streaked through the forest, this time sounding like riotous thunder instead of tinkling rain in her haste to escape.

CHAPTER 9

*W*ayland

"How was your night?" Wayland asked Red Claw on their trek to Wayland's favorite hunting area, near an outcropping of rocks where animals often lounged.

"That witch Suze is dynamite in the sack," the coyote shifter exclaimed.

"Glad you enjoyed yourself." Wayland grinned, and pointed to Red Claw's massive head. "Your crow feathers are sideways and upside down in the braids."

"Oops!" The shifter adjusted them. "So, thanks for the introduction. You've gone above and beyond. I'd like to see her again. She was super fun to talk to."

"Happy to play matchmaker."

"How was *your* night?" Red Claw glanced over at Wayland. "You turned in early."

"Yeah, sometimes a guy is just beat." He was bummed by Stormy's unexpected departure, but decided it was for the best. The coyotes could be prone to gossip, and if a racy tidbit about Stormy leaked to the Tundra pack, it would surely wreak havoc.

He and Red Claw reached the stone outcropping. Sure enough, a stag was sunning there. Red Claw used a patchwork of howls and low yips to confuse the deer while Wayland silently stalked. His serious case of blue balls from the fiery encounter with Stormy fueled his aggressive charge, and he sunk his talon-like claws in the stag's ribs before delivering a ferocious bite to its jugular.

Working together, the two shifters were able to not only bag the hefty stag, but three snarly badgers and armfuls of fat grouse as well. They shifted to their human forms to carry the food on their massive shoulders.

"Who knew there was still so much game in these over-hunted woods?" Red Claw marveled on their way to the coyote den with the kills. "We're good tag team, boss."

"We are. We'll make an even better martial force," Wayland added.

"Yes. Only a few less than enthusiastic coyote shifters, and I'll work on them. How much longer 'til we take on the Tundra?" Red Claw asked.

"Another week or two is all. I'll make an announcement when we eat."

"I see Ice Lake." Red Claw pointed up ahead. "It's not far now."

Wayland said wistfully, "You guys are right behind where the Leblancs once lived."

"The good old days," Red Claw mused. "We coyotes took shelter here from our original spot by Snow Mountain, when they cleared the forest to build that damn Lodge."

They reached the coyote den, in a hollow filled with blackberry bushes and Lodgepole Pine. Not a moment too soon, as the haul, slung over their shoulders, had gotten quite heavy.

The coyote pack broke out in raucous cheers at the sight of fresh meat. Wayland and Red Claw arranged the bounty on burdock leaves while the hungry pack circled around. The women brought out baskets of blackberries, mixed greens, and pitchers of spiked punch.

Females and the young went first, then the adult males. Bones gave Berry, his mate, a peck on the cheek then came over to stand with Wayland and Red Claw. She stood tall like Bones and shared his friendly manner, waving to Wayland with a dimpled grin. Wayland hoped he would find another mate who fit his own disposition so well. Stormy's image wafted in, but he pushed it out.

Dangerous liaison.

Bones sat with his rangy torso sloped over his wiry legs and cut into the venison. "Thanks, Wayland, for the help you've given us. This feast is impressive."

Wayland cocked his head toward Red Claw, who was digging into a grouse thigh. "Red Claw was saying that we make a fierce hunting team and I agree."

"Nice! Hopefully, we'll all make as fierce a team when we fight the Tundra," said Bones, echoing Wayland's earlier sentiment. "One talent I have is to pick up and send signals with my visioning. Kind of like pictures with messages."

"That could come in quite handy."

Other alphas joined them on a reed-woven rug.

"I really appreciate you guys," Wayland told Bones, gnawing on a flank of venison. "It's nice to have pack allies when you're alone in the Canadian wilderness."

Bones tossed the long bone into the fire and clapped Wayland on the back. "Our pleasure, shifter. You're an upstanding guy. Come join us for a drink and a chat anytime."

"And a war," Red Claw reminded them all, holding up his punch. "We're in this together. The Tundra pack needs some serious payback for slaughtering your own, for flirting with our females, for overhunting the land, and being arrogant A-holes."

When the feast was finished and the pack sat back, satiated, Wayland stood to make an announcement. "The battle will commence in about eight days, so practice hard and keep your body and wits sharp!"

"Hell yasss!" a rallying cry went up amongst the coyotes, followed by boisterous, bloodthirsty howls.

With a date set, the anticipation was like electric charges during a thunderstorm.

The alpha coyotes moved closer on the mats to talk strategy.

"Already we've run a handful of mock battles," Bones explained. "The maze of hidey-holes around our lair for our special Whack-a-Mole style guerilla warfare is working well in trial runs."

"In the real battles, the concealed pits will function as traps and obstacle courses for the uninitiated Tundra," another alpha clarified.

"Perfect!" Wayland exclaimed. "We want those fuckers confused as hell so we can charge in, and whack or whip 'em before they figure out what hit 'em." The group broke out in rough laughter. "So, have you started to dig the trenches near where we'll be fighting?"

"Yeah, boss," said Red Claw, his cheeks growing ruddy from the hooch. "Our guys have been getting up before dawn while those lazy Tundra sleep in." More laughter, though Wayland knew Red Claw had slept in with Suze just this morning.

Wayland and Bones had already decided the actual battle would be fought partly around Ice Lake and partly around the Tundra den. But, of course, there was no way they could practice at these locations. Even here, coyote scouts constantly searched the den's perimeter for Tundra spies.

* * *

WHEN WAYLAND RETURNED to his camp, his muscles were sore from the hunt and his mind weary from strategizing and poring over diagrams. But he was happy at all he accomplished. He pulled off his boots, jeans, and T-shirt, and lounged on his bed, still mussed from his and Stormy's halted tryst. He inhaled deeply, luxuriating in her lingering floral scent. Stretching out, he wished she were sharing his bed. How would he be able to stand not seeing her for days?

How would he learn to stay away for good? Another pressing question, when it dawned on him more every day she was the Juliet to his Romeo. Star-crossed meant fated for bad luck, didn't it? So, if they become a couple, it was fated both would perish. Wayland thought of getting another Tarot reading to settle the matter, but he was too weary to socialize with Suze and Jacey. His life was getting too tangled with contrasting loyalties—Stormy versus Jacey, Thorn versus Stormy, Wayland versus Thorn.

His eyes landed on an object that made his heart jump—the map he'd unearthed at the abandoned Tundra den was still on a shelf at the end of the bed, where he'd placed it weeks ago.

How could he have forgotten about it? A map might provide valuable insight into the Tundra mind. It might lead to another Tundra den, even help defeat the bastards!

He leapt up and grabbed the map, then laid back down, and unrolled it, dust from the old Tundra den sifting through the air, making him sneeze.

Curiously, it highlighted a meandering route, past Snow

Mountain and up to the higher peaks, where the snow never melted…the part of Canada that was still true wilderness, not these tired stomping grounds forcibly cut into sections by hipster lodges, cell phone towers, and suburban sprawl.

He'd never heard of the few tiny towns on the trail map— or should he call them outposts? Or hamlets, like in old fairytales?

Gray Fiord was one, Angel's Dome another. But it was the hamlet of Winter Crow that set Wayland's pulse rattling— because someone had circled it with red ink. He did some quick calculations on his laptop, and figured he could make it there and back in four or five days, if he hurried.

It was a good time for a break. He couldn't chance running into Stormy, or God forbid, her taking the risk to visit him again before the battle. His coyote allies were practicing their war drills without him anyway. They had Bones, a smart, seasoned co-commander. Besides, Wayland would be back before the battle to finalize plans with Bones.

Tracking down what that red circle on the map meant could grant him the special sauce to help him overcome the Tundra, once and for all. He threw the essentials in his backpack, including a ton of venison chews and the bottle of Red Claw's blackberry hooch. He packed a jacket, a wool hat, gloves, and a compass, because he'd never climbed peaks high as the ones he might face on this journey. Finally, he packed the weighty stuff he saved for the most ominous situations—explosive charges, handcuffs, a scythe, sleeping pills, and some nasty elixirs—because he wanted to return alive.

CHAPTER 10

 **tormy**

It was only mid-morning, but Stormy was at World's Edge anyway. She was a mess of nerves since that rude coyote had rapped on Wayland's door, making a racket and scaring the crap out of her. Not to mention, he interrupted a hot make-out session with Wayland. The way he used his tongue, his rough-hewn hands along her hips—holy freaking moon-fire! She hadn't intended for that to happen.

Together they made a hazardous brew, like mixing tequila with beer.

She brushed back her long hair, not caring that it was tangled from rolling in his bed and wet with dew from racing through the forest. Then she took a long pull of her blueberry vodka and chewed on the garnish, a sprig of thyme. She wasn't a big drinker, but she needed something to quell her sense of approaching trouble. She liked that the pleasing blueberry flavor outplayed the alcohol.

World's Edge was dark and practically empty. The pool cues were lined up along the wall, and the small round tables were tidy and ready for customers. Grayish blue light from the overcast sky filtered through the drawn shades. It was perfect for her mood. She didn't recognize the bartender, but he was capable enough, the way he'd mixed her drink.

"You new here?" she asked him, eying his corduroy jeans and button-down shirt, a bit hokey for this bar.

"Yeah, I trained last week." He regarded her with pale blue eyes. "I haven't seen you around either."

"I've been pretty busy." She took another sip. "What's happening? Any juicy news?" She may as well play spy. Not for any particular side, just to stay informed.

He shrugged. "I've heard that the Tundra are training."

"For what?" She tensed, though she did her best to sound unfazed.

"Some upcoming battle against the coyotes? Or someone who's giving them trouble? Trying to get too cozy with one of their female royals?" He shrugged and began to fill bowls of nuts along the long counter. "You can imagine I hear bits and pieces, so it's not always easy to patch it together."

"I get it, sure. Are you Tundra?"

"No, I'm a Windrunner. I try to stay neutral." He gave her a toothy smile. Ah, she saw it now. The Windrunners did have prominent teeth. "You?" he asked her.

She was surprised he didn't know Thorn, or that he was her brother. Thorn was a notorious alpha around here. *Just as well.* "I'm a random shifter who likes her late-morning cocktail." She held it up and guzzled.

"Kudos to that. A top off?" The server held the vodka above her glass, and she nodded. He poured in a liberal amount and said cheerfully, "On the house, just for the heck of it."

"Thanks."

A coyote shifter in a tattered jacket wandered in, solo. Even in human form, she could tell them by their shaggy hair, hungry stares, and rough manners. He sat one barstool over and ordered a beer. The bartender served him before wandering to the other end of the bar to wash beer mugs.

The coyote shifter grunted, assessing her. "They're fighting over you, I hear."

What? Shut the hell up! Why would you say this out loud, among other shifters or even in this bar at all?

"I don't know what you're talking about," she said finally, shaking her head.

"My fellow shifters are putting their lives on the line for you," he groused. "What did you ever do for us?"

She couldn't stop herself from asking, "Are you in Bones' pack or...?"

Within half a second, a throng of burly Tundra shifters crashed through the doors, seized Stormy by the arms, and began to drag her out, kicking and screaming. They seized the disgruntled coyote as well, who yelled a string of nasty expletives not only at his captors, but at Stormy. "Mother fuckin' bastard royals! You're a bunch of arrogant SOBs, and your entitled lush of a she-wolf wench can go drown in the damn lake!"

Stormy had her own battles. "Lay off, Tundras! You've got the wrong shifter!" she shouted, struggling to free her arms from their vice grips. She didn't recognize them; they must be third tier wannabes, however burly. "Hey!" she shouted, "I'm Thorn's sister! I'm part of your own pack, you fools!" She struggled mightily, to no avail. "Bartender!" she tried next. "Call the Ice Lake vigilantes! Call your Windrunners! Please, help!"

She shuddered when the bartender leveled an icy stare at her and announced, "The Tundra alphas paid me a ton more cash to pretend I was a Windrunner and chat you up than you shelled out for your vodka cocktail and lousy-ass tip." Then he strolled out of the side exit.

The Tundra thugs cuffed and dragged her from World's Edge and into the backseat of a metal paddy wagon she'd never seen before. Where had they gotten this? It looked like a tricked out giant ATV. Was this Thorn's doing? A shifter crowded in on each side of her, their eyes turning into the chiseled diamond glower of the turned Tundra werewolf.

Is this for real or am I having a nightmare?

When she started to howl, one of them snapped a ball gag around her mouth. She stomped with all her might on his foot. He yowled and jabbed her mercilessly in the ribs with a nightstick.

This pain is no dream. It hurts like holy hell!

The other shifter sunk a syringe in her arm and drove the liquid all the way in. She faded out, seeing the metal bolts of the tank whirling ahead of her, and her blue butterfly familiars plummeting out of eyesight.

* * *

STORMY WOKE with another merciless headache and a throbbing in her side. It was pitch dark. She tried to feel the sore area, near her left hip, but both arms were tied to a hard pallet. The place stunk of piss, mildew, and rat feces. She coughed, trying to dispel the stench.

Closing her eyes, she strained to conjure her butterfly familiars. Had they—whoever they were—destroyed her tiny companions as well? Tears sprang to her eyes, and a helpless anger followed. Who would do this to her? Was there a third enemy stalking them all that bribed a few Tundras with big money? Someone who hated Thorn, Wayland, and even the coyote shifters? The possibility was terrifying. She lifted her head and searched in the dark for any pinpoints of light. Any sign of life. With a wave of dizziness, she reeled back, and her head hit the hard pallet.

* * *

"I TOLD you there'd be consequences," a familiar voice was saying, from the end of what sounded like a long tunnel. "You never listen. You're never careful. You don't care about anything but yourself. Or that guy."

Thorn! It was Thorn talking. Her eyes fluttered open. There was just enough light from a lantern to make out his seated shape—hefty, long-armed, and hunched. She groaned and shuffled her legs to indicate she couldn't speak. Just in case he wanted a response.

"Get that ball gag off!" he ordered to someone she couldn't see.

The moment the restraint was off, she gulped air. Even foul air was life giving. Then she laid into her demented brother. "What the hell do you think you're doing?"

"Putting you in a place where you can't interfere. You're your own worst enemy, sister. I know everything. You're humping that guy who wants to kill me—kill all of us!"

"I'm not banging him, you disgusting shit!"

"Banging, palling around like moony lovebirds. What's the difference? How could you be so heartless and clueless? The dude wants to wipe us from the face of the earth, Stormy! He doesn't care about you! He'll cut your throat as easily as he'll cut mine, and every one of our Tundra brethren. Wake up!"

Wayland won't do that. There's a real connection between us. He wants to keep me safe. We've kissed and held each other. Would he really turn on me?

"You lie!" Stormy hissed. "You're just jealous of his *real* nobility."

Thorn slapped her hard across the face. It smarted, but she didn't give him the pleasure of groaning. "You were supposed to give us information, not canoodle with the enemy. My spies saw you at that campsite. We saw the whole damn cuddle scene. So revolting."

Stormy's throat seized up as if it was Thorn strangling her. It was terror, pure terror for Wayland. How could she have been so naïve to think her brother wouldn't track her every move? She should never have gone to Wayland's campsite. Thorn might harm her, but he wouldn't kill her. But that so-called courtesy wouldn't extend to Wayland. "Get me out of here. Remove the rusty handcuffs, *brother*." She uttered this last word with precision, like a sharpened blade going through flesh.

He towered over her, his eyes gleaming maniacally in the dim light. "I'll leave you here a while longer. I don't trust you. You're as dangerous as that oaf you're stalking. Enjoy the rats. They seem kind of hungry." The sound of his chuckle jangled over the odd clink-clank music of the old lock. Where had she heard that before?

In the Tundra's old metal-lined underground prison...the one beneath their abandoned den!

Her skin prickled. She doubted she would be able to throw her spirit from all the way down here. She remembered trying to astral project from here long ago. It hadn't worked. How would she be able to warn Wayland? Warn the witches next-door to him at the campsite if need be? These were her frantic wonderings before she faded once more.

CHAPTER 11

Wayland

WAYLAND HAD PASSED through Angel's Dome, a picture post-card village of log cabins, each with its puffing stone chimney and circle of beleaguered evergreens, and was nearing Gray Fiord when it started snowing in earnest. It had already been two days of hiking with no sleep. His feet were blistered and his face raw and pocked from last night's pounding hailstorm. At least the daytime snow didn't cause open sores. Wayland's pulse beat like a fated timer ticking down to a zero point. So far, he'd been unwilling to stop, but he was exhausted. He would need shelter if he intended to save a speck of energy to climb the last peaks to Winter Crow, which was a daunting 50 more miles, straight up snow-covered rock faces.

So, he ventured into the Flintlock Inn, a green clapboard place with a tin roof and rustic lanterns aglow in the front windows. He paid for a room and took a seat in their dimly lit bar, empty of customers. "A double shot of bourbon," Wayland growled.

The bartender, a brown-bearded man in a bulky wool sweater, obliged. He regarded Wayland with deeply set dark eyes. "Where'd you come from, mister? Looks like you got pelted with buckshot."

"Oh that—holes in my damn face. I got caught in a hailstorm."

"And you didn't take cover?" The man sounded incredulous.

"No time." Wayland gulped his bourbon and cringed. "Woo! The burn of this alcohol sure feels better than the sting of that rock-hard hail."

The bartender laughed and poured him another. "Where are you headed?" He paused when he saw Wayland frown. "That is, if you don't mind me asking?"

"Oh, I may pass through Winter Crow. Curiosity, voyaging, just for shits and giggles."

"Why that godforsaken place?" The bartender rolled his eyes.

"What's so bad about it?" Wayland's nerves jangled even though he'd gotten some relief from the tranquilizing lull of the bourbon. "What's the problem?"

"No one goes there, is all. There's no businesses or tourism or even a darn café." The bartender sniggered. "The place fits the name."

"Care to explain?"

"Most crows fly south in winter," the guy replied, resting a hand on the counter. "But some crows? Well, a few of them stay, but only the wounded ones, the stubborn ones, the strange ones." He gave another horsey snort. "I'd say Winter Crow has a few of the strange ones."

"Anyone in particular?" Wayland leaned forward on his elbows.

"Well, they say there's a witch trapped up there. A crafty black crow."

Wayland's gut pinched hard, almost as bad as his appendicitis attack before they'd removed it. "Another shot, please. Keep the change." He threw cash down on the bar. The server refilled his shot glass. "Well, what about the rumors? Is there really a…witch up there?" Wayland's throat caught on the word.

"Nah." The bartender waved his hand dismissively. "You know how nutty folks get with their superstitions and whatnot." He broke out in gravelly laughter. "These mountain people are some frosty, flea-bitten crows, they are. All of 'em if you ask me." He slid a menu over Wayland's way. "You wanna soak up all that bourbon with some home cookin', eh?"

"Whatcha got?"

"Bison stew, fish stew, caribou liver stew… Well I guess we're just brimming with stews to warm up the frozen bones."

"Bison stew sounds good."

The food was too tasty to chat and chew, and besides, the bartender shuffled back to his post on a stool by the side door, so the conversation was effectively over. Once Wayland's belly was filled with hot, nutritious food an overwhelming fatigue overcame him and he retired to his room. He managed two hours of sleep, but then awoke, a bundle of worries.

He lay sleepless on the inn's over-firm mattress and stared out the window at the snow piling up. How would he find the so-called witch, or red-circled treasure, whatever it was on that hidden map, without any people or inns or businesses in town to ask leading questions to? He wondered if he should've asked the bartender if he'd heard of the Tundra pack, and if there were Tundra up in Winter Crow.

On second thought, it was for the best. One never knew how many spies the Tundra had, or if this so-called bartender was hired by them to alert their spies already waiting for him in Winter fucking Crow.

He felt an ache of a different sort. "Stormy," he murmured. "I need you." He listened to how that sounded, and realized he'd never said that to anyone, or even admitted it to himself. Need had only existed as a craving for food, or sex, or drink.

Needing a human for company, or simply to lie warm by his side in solidarity was different.

That was big.

He felt the prick of tears and wiped them away.

Finally, he closed his eyes, forced himself to unclench his bunched muscles and picture his worries drifting off in a fast-moving creek.

* * *

THE BLIZZARD DROVE on relentlessly outside his window when he awoke the next morning. He'd gotten to sleep after all, and he was glad for it. He used some of the salve in his pack to spread over the worst of the raw facial wounds, and donned his ski jacket over his sweater, pulling his gloves as far as he could under the cuffs. Then he struggled out and up the mountain.

By afternoon, the trail markers were covered with towering mounds of snow that he had to bat off to determine the way forward. At least he had his compass and the simple trail map. He stopped for only ten minutes to wolf down a hunk of venison jerky and wash it down with blackberry hooch.

He wondered how Bones and Red Claw were doing at the coyote compound. He smiled at the thought of them. Allies were gifts to be grateful for. And here, in this punishing place, the mere thought of them warmed his soul and renewed his strength.

The final ten miles were almost vertical on slick, snow-covered boulders. He fell more times than he could count and slid down the rock faces, only to pick himself up and wearily retrace his steps.

The blizzard finally slowed to a steady white pelting, but during the last two miles something else worried him. He swore he saw flashes of movement in his side vision. Was a mountain lion stalking him, or something worse?

A Tundra assassin?

His senses were on high alert, and he was primed to transform to his full werewolf form if need be. He inhaled deeply, using his supernatural scenting and visioning ability to ascertain the nature of the danger.

Most Tundra stank of the gnarly blood of the fisher cats they were partial to eating, and the fermented, ancient sediment found three or four layers underground in their cavernous subterranean dens. He smelled nothing like this. Could they be bundled in so many subzero coat layers they had no scent? Or was he was getting paranoid? In a place like this, it paid to be paranoid. He drove on.

Finally, through a blur of white, blown on a frigid wind, he saw what looked to be city gates. Yes! Trudging closer, he saw them clearly—gothic wrought-iron style, with a matching fence surrounding the village, like in a medieval fantasy book. Above the imposing entrance gate was a sign, also in wrought iron, that spelled out 'Winter Crow' in scrolled script.

Wayland almost fell to his knees at the sight, partly out of sheer relief and partly from exhaustion. He dragged himself through the gates and down the main street—if you could call it that.

The bartender back at the Flintlock Inn wasn't lying. The few storefronts still standing were boarded up. There were collapsed structures and empty lots, but no inns with window lanterns or even a single flickering candle to welcome travelers. There was one lane with a crooked street sign that said 'Main Street'. Granted, it was still snowing, but Wayland saw nary a soul.

He peered up narrow side streets that were really just snow-covered paths. After a few minutes' walk, he spotted one house to the right, but no chimney wafting out smoke. No lights in the windows. No sign of humanity.

He trudged on. A few more cottages lay to either side of the path, but again, no lights glowed from within, and there were no cars or snowplows or anyone shoveling from without. It reminded him of the darkest, most forbidding drawings of Van Gogh's that he'd seen in a library book long ago. Snowy peasant villages without light, without hope.

"Why on earth did the Tundra bother to hide this funky trail map?" he muttered to himself, curling the map with his gloved hands. "It seems pretty useless."

Taking cover under a shuttered storefront he pored over the map, trying to see if the red-circled area was on a street whose name he had overlooked. The lines were smudgy— from how many fingerprints? But this time, he detected a faint scribble. He narrowed his eyes in a valiant attempt to read it.

Sanctuary Road.

Curious. Again, there was a flash of movement to his right, a blue blur. He swung around to see an ancient woman in a hooded wool coat—patched and re-patched—hobbling along with the help of her cane. He almost laughed out loud. Was *she* what he was so scared of when he saw movement on the trail up here? But who knew? She could be a Tundra spy as easily as a hulking muscle man could.

Eyeing the woman's blue cloth bag, filled to the breaking point with candles of every size and color, he wondered where she'd come from, since everything was boarded up, and where she was headed. "May I help you carry your satchel?" he asked her, as gentle a tone as he could muster.

She gave him a wrinkly grin. "Oh, sonny, I'm used to the storms."

"Just thought I'd ask. Where is everyone around here?" asked Wayland.

"It's a small town. We like it small."

"Who likes it small? What kinds of folks live around here?"

"The crows," she replied. "Less crows mean more perches."

Wayland's skin crawled. Was this more than just a local joke? Was this code for Leave the Tundra's Secret Retreat Alone? No! He must resist his growing paranoia. Maybe he should just blurt the silent parts out loud. Ask the big questions. She was just someone's granny after all, and she was shuffling away. Another minute and he would miss his chance.

He scurried forward and stood in front of her so she couldn't continue without swerving around him. "Look, I need to know if you've ever heard of the Tundra."

Her white brows crossed. "The Tundra? Is that a type of tree?"

"No. It's not a tree." He sighed. "Ever heard of a witch around here? The bartender back in Gray Fiord at the Flintlock Inn said there was a witch up here. He called her a black crow. Does that make any sense to you?" He spoke slowly and clearly to make sure she got every word.

"The witch has a dog shelter up Sanctuary Road," the woman replied matter-of-factly.

"Dog shelter?" he echoed, his jaw gaping. This just got

more peculiar with every passing minute. What in the world would Thorn and Ransom and the Tundra thugs want with a spooky crone and her dog shelter?

"You heard me," the woman fired back. She tried to veer past Wayland but he trotted backward just ahead of her so she couldn't avoid stopping again. "Let me by. I'm late to deliver my candles."

"You make them yourself? They're pretty." She nodded and smiled, showing gaps where teeth had been. "Just one more question!" Wayland asked. "Whose dogs are they?"

"Strays who wandered from the paths," she said quizzically and took on a wistful look. "I'd love me a lapdog to cuddle, but not them dogs. They bite. They'll take your arm off." She tapped him with her cane and he let her by.

Wayland watched her trudge up the hill and off somewhere to the left, down a pitch-dark lane that seemed abandoned. He glanced at his map. That street was labeled Candle Lane. "Good grief!" he mumbled. "I never thought an old lady would weird me out." With that, he bucked the rucksack up on his shoulders, shook snow from his coat, and set off up Sanctuary Road.

He must've walked another two miles when he came to a hovel with an imposing iron fence around it. It was still snowing and already quite gray, and with dusk upon him he could barely see. He took a flashlight from his pack and shone it on the fence. Out of nowhere, slavering dogs with pointy fangs similar to those of turned werewolves charged at him with such ferocity that many smashed into the fence, and kept on smashing and barking.

"This is it?" Wayland muttered. "The place the Tundra thought was so important they had to hide the map?" He crept closer, inspiring another mad round of furious growling and barking. These dogs were enormous—part mastiff or Russian wolfhound, or… He wondered what the hell they were. "Part fucking monster," he decided.

His werewolf side was eager to come out and play, and scare the holy crap out of these hounds from hell. But more than scare them, he needed to earn their trust or otherwise render them tame. If he just scared them like they were scaring him, there would be a fierce standoff he would have to be on guard for, and he would never be able to concentrate on getting inside the compound or whatever the fuck this creepy-ass place was. "Sanctuary, huh? Shelter, huh?" he murmured, more to himself than to the slavering beasts.

A plan formed, whole hog. He shrugged his pack off his shoulders and took out supplies. He rolled up piece after piece of the venison, each with a tablet inside it. "Let's hope these sleeping pills are good for something after all," he mumbled, folding the last piece of venison. The hounds, smelling the smoked meat, were now leaping at the fence, howling, and drooling their whiskered muzzles off.

Even wearing thick gloves, Wayland figured he'd have to be extremely cautious to not get his hands chomped off when he doled out the treats. So, transforming to werewolf had its perks, if it inspired fear to tamp down the dogs' aggressive snapping at the food.

Wayland allowed his body to turn. First, his chest swelled to monstrous proportions, then his hands sprouted claws three times the size and deadlier than the feral hounds', which caused his gloves to rip and fall. Finally his head and neck thickened. He was glad his sweater, sweatpants, and jacket stretched, or they also would've split at the seams. His eyes, now a glowing gold, unnerved the dogs enough to shut their traps and back off. It was, hopefully, enough time for Wayland to approach the fence and fork over the first treat. The boldest dog, with a neck like a 50-year old maple trunk, inched forward, lunged for the loaded jerky through the iron bars, and gobbled it down.

"Good dog!" Wayland exclaimed. "More doggie treats, Fidos!" he called to the others. The first hound getting food broke the intimidation spell. All fifteen by Wayland's count, rushed the fence and gulped down a tainted treat. They barked and howled for more.

"Now we wait for you to go nighty-night!" Wayland growled back at them. He was still in werewolf mode, his eyes glowing like neon signs, and the dogs again backed up. Wayland sat on his pack and shook snow off his hood and boots. Normally, it took Wayland at least half an hour to feel the fuzzy, lulling effects of the sedative. With this pack of canines, he figured it was only fifteen minutes before every last Fido was snoring sloppily, flanks and forelegs splayed over the snow. These hounds might be huge attack dogs on steroids, but when it came to pills, they were toy-poodle lightweights.

No time to waste. Who knew how long they'd be out of it? Wayland found a spot toward the back of the property where the fence was tilting out and decided to scale it. He was halfway up when something leapt on him.

The next thing he knew, he was fighting for his life with a werewolf similar in size and stinking of stale fisher cat blood.

A freaking Tundra!

He had to kill the damn thing. He could not let word of his arrival get back to Ice Lake, or everyone he cared for would be dead. The Tundra bit deeply and viciously into Wayland's arm, causing blood to spread like a red sea over his sweater and jacket. He, in turn, dug his werewolf's claws, akin to jackknives, into the Tundra werewolf's ribs. In a downward thrust, he carved rows of jagged wounds. The Tundra moaned, but went wild on Wayland's already injured face, reopening the pocks from the hailstorm, and ripping his ear half off.

Wayland renewed his efforts, though his ear hung by a mere strip. With a quick swipe, he snapped the fleshy string that connected his ear to his head and thrust the ear in a secret pocket inside his sweater. Then he kneed the attacker with full force in the crotch. The Tundra writhed in helpless pain. This gave Wayland enough time to land fatal blows to the werewolf's temples with each of his fists.

After the Tundra had drawn his last breath, Wayland took a moment to sniff the icy air, searching for other Tundra stink. How had he missed their notorious odor before? The venison jerky must've drowned it out. He also searched with his supernatural visioning.

He found nothing but hound breath, heavy with venison jerky. It surprised him that the Tundra had only installed one guard to this frigid outpost. Nevertheless, it must hold more important treasure than he imagined.

Without hesitation, Wayland scaled the fence, using his claws like boot crampons. Once on top, he leapt to the ground and peered to where the dogs lay, still asleep. He approached the hovel, which looked like nothing more than a large and disheveled garden shed. But now that he knew for certain it was the Tundra's, he realized there might well be a lot more than met the eye. They were experts at building underground dens.

Shining his flashlight on various parts of the cottage, he located the door. It might be a humble abode, but the metal walls and door were fortified like a military tank. He tried to pick the lock with a long switchblade. Nothing doing. He put his full werewolf muscle into it, battering it with one side of his locked and loaded torso. The door didn't budge, though it clanked loudly.

He groaned, distracted by intense pain. His arm throbbed,

and his ear, or what was left of it, was bleeding all over him. He needed to do something, or soon the spouting liquid would cool and freeze, transforming him, werewolf or human, into a fucking iceberg. He reached in his pack for a bandana, and wrapped it like a skintight turban around his skull. The ear would have to be sewn on later—or not. He pulled it from inside his sweater, stuck it in a small collection jar, and then put the jar in his pack. Once again, he checked the hounds for any movement, then the surroundings for any more Tundra. Nothing. So, if he had to make a louder noise, say blowing something up, no one would come running. After all, he'd hiked in quite a distance from where he'd seen the lone old lady.

He took the smallest of his explosive charges, calculated down to the exact milligram needed to blast down a door without injuring anyone inside, set it in place with tape, lit the fuse, and rapidly lurched backward before it blew.

The deafening boom and its sudden light had a few of the dogs shuffling in their sleep, but thankfully they didn't fully awaken. Wayland transformed to human form to fit through the singed doorway and walked down a sloping ramp leading to an underground lair.

"What is this?" a female voice called out. "Have you come here to kill me?"

 tormy

"WAKE UP! Snap out of it, sister," Thorn implored. "Come, eat!"

She shuddered, angered by the sound of Thorn's voice, yet relieved to be alive. Her stomach growled at the aroma of grilled rabbit, her favorite.

"I've cooked you a treat," he said as he switched on a wall lantern. "Sit up. I've done what you asked and unfastened the binds. Here you go." He moved a chair closer to her so she could hoist herself up on it.

In fact, her bones ached from being strapped down for so many hours. She struggled to her feet and sat, and glared at Thorn, who was making a fanfare of setting her feast on the table. He slowly lifted the silver casserole top to reveal the steamy rabbit with an apple in its maw, and then poured a goblet of pink Cloudberry wine, her favored drink. Even though she was furious at Thorn, she couldn't help but salivate over the profusion of treats.

He watched her gobble down the dinner in tense silence.

"You better let me out," she snapped, after eating her fill of the rabbit. "So, you're done being a royal ass to me?"

He shrugged. "You're my sister, and part of my royal line, Stormy dear."

"Don't call me dear. Just open the damn door. I'll let myself out." She swept the neatly folded linen napkin across her greasy mouth and threw it down on the pile of rabbit bones.

"What am I to call you, sister?" he asked wearily, still ignoring her demand for freedom.

"Don't be ridiculous, Thorn!" she shouted. "Open that door. Now!"

"I might." His brow furrowed. "But first, tell me where Wayland went."

Stormy flinched. The sweet wine abruptly turned sour in her stomach. Wayland was gone? Had he decided to head back to Louisiana? Not wreak revenge? Not fight for justice for his dead mate?

Not fight for me, for my heart—

She remembered that disgruntled coyote at World's Edge insisted that's what Wayland was fighting for. It had kept her hoping.

Stormy ran a hand across her lips, remembering Wayland's tender kiss, the heat of his body, and how his heart beat hard against her soft chest. The thought of never seeing him again weighed her down, made her hunch over. But she had to snap out of this dizzying pain. Play it cool around Thorn.

She blurted a line that would put him off his own con. "Wayland went back to the USA. He decided to let you live. His camper is still there as a decoy. He ditched it, brother.

The fight wasn't worth it. So, I guess you better just forget about your war fantasies. Just tell your Tundra guys to stop practicing their knife throws, all of that mad somersaulting. Sorry to disappoint you." She suppressed a snicker.

The look of befuddlement on Thorn's face was infinitely satisfying. Although she was totally making it up, who knew? It could be true. At the very least, it would stop Thorn from searching for Wayland. It would give Wayland time to do whatever he needed, and send Thorn back to the drawing board regarding his next move.

She would always be a Tundra royal; she was proud of that. Yet something had shifted in her. She had decided to trust Wayland, to protect him, no matter what he decided to do, even if she never saw him again. That gave Stormy a calm in the face of uncertainty, a steely resolve like the deeper waters of Ice Lake: chilly, steady, and dark with mysterious power.

Thorn leapt up and leaned close to her face. "You're lying!" His nostrils flared in fury, exposing a tangle of nose hairs. He'd been drinking a lot, and it wasn't a good look. Veins in his cheeks rose like red spider webs.

"He's gone," Stormy repeated, and again, "He's gone." She attempted to walk toward the metal door. Thorn grabbed her by the arm. She spun around and shook free, a bolt of fierce hatred driving her. "Don't touch me."

He stood against the door, blocking her way. She reached beyond him for the latch and jiggled it. Locked. "I know where I am. In the old Tundra prison! Why'd you put me in this metal cage? What is wrong with you, Thorn?" she screamed right in his ear. He flinched. Good. She'd hurt his eardrum. She yelled, even louder this time, aiming to do worse damage. "Answer me, Thorn! Why am I in this goddamn metal box?"

He broke away, fists balled into weapons, and clearly

trying to control his rising temper and not smash her face in. Then, legs akimbo, fists still balled, he said, "So you can't play your fancy moon flying games."

"What the hell are you even talking about, Thorn?"

He's scared I'll astral travel. That's it! How does he know what I do?

"That's what you called it when you were a kid—your fancy flying games. I haven't forgotten." He glared at her, and she saw in his glower a simmering fear. He was afraid of her powers. How in the world had he found out she was still practicing her craft? She'd kept it under the radar for many, many years now. What, exactly, did he worry she would do with them?

She laughed, low and threatening. "Who's losing it now, brother? Do you hear yourself? You sound crazy. Those were the childish games of a seven-year-old girl, not serious things. What even made you think of them? Are you afraid of me, or what?" She laughed again and threw up her hands. "Look, I'm just a sheltered Tundra, one of the purebred Tundra pack queens, as you always say. I'm not a wild, evil witch or anything!"

He joined in the laughter, but in it, she heard a trembling. She'd struck a nerve, and she knew it. But that did no good to help convince him to free her.

"A deal is a deal, Thorn," she reminded him in a kinder tone. "You told me you'd let me out if I told you where Wayland went. And I did."

"Yeah, um… No deal." With that, he rushed out so fast and relocked the door with the *clickety clack* of its rusty lock, that she had no time to grab his arm or even yank his hair.

She plunked down on the thin pallet and threw her head in her hands.

Stormy waited patiently, many hours, for the moon to rise. She could feel its ascension in her gut, like the lilting of hope. "Fancy moon travel, eh? I'm older. Maybe my power has grown stronger than these metal walls!" she mumbled. "Maybe my spirit can find a chink in the wall to pass through." She lay on her back, closed her eyes, and breathed deeply, steadily, sinking into the lucid dreaming state that prompted her travels.

She pictured Wayland and who might be near him. All she got was the memory of his kiss, which fizzled away like smoke in rain. Frustrated, she tried to picture Jacey. Those had been easy astral flights, though she'd told herself she wouldn't put Jacey through them again. But a dire situation called for a suspension of civil boundaries. She breathed and imagined, but couldn't get her spirit to go further than smooshed up against the ceiling of the metal cage—butter trying to penetrate stone.

Somehow, this damn metal still traps my astral spirit. But how in the blessed goddess's moon could my brother know this?

Her body clenched in clammy dread. How could he know more than she did about her own unique magic?

CHAPTER 13

Wayland

HE TROOPED STEADILY down the narrow ramp toward a flickering light and wondered what he would say. How would he pacify this person in case she had a weapon already aimed at his head, or had the supernatural power to transform him to liquid before pouring him down a drain? Could she burn him alive?

"Who are you?" she called from the light ahead in an unnaturally high squeak. "Are you Tundra, or from Winter Crow, or what?"

"Neither. I came from far away. I'm not here to harm you. Please, put down any weapons. Let me explain why I'm here before you react." He walked the last few steps into the light, and saw her.

"Weapons? I need no guns or swords to harm you." An imposing woman with a straight, narrow nose and flowing white hair that reached her hips faced him. Was she sixty or seventy or what? It was hard to tell; she had an ageless quality. Her gown was crimson, and its length gave her the appearance of being taller than she probably was. Her regal, dark-eyed presence seemed oddly familiar. She regarded him solemnly, without flinching. In her hand, she held a carved wooden staff about a foot long. She raised it at him. "If you're not Tundra, how did you get past the dogs?"

"I'll answer any question, but first, may I enter?" He had to be polite to get in her good graces, and show her an alpha could restrain himself. He had to prove she need not attack him like the hounds above ground had wanted to.

She pointed with her staff to a small parlor, also decorated in dark crimson. He walked slowly, to show her he was safe.

"Sit," she ordered. He complied, sitting gingerly on a velvet-upholstered chair with leaf carvings on the armrests. "So, who are you then?" She sat in a tall-backed chair facing him and rested her staff against it. A massive hound, like the ones he'd drugged, padded in from a side door and sniffed Wayland's hand. He lurched back, expecting a ferocious bite. The dog, all one hundred pounds of it, sauntered over to the woman and lay at her feet.

"The dog… He didn't…?"

"My dog, Knight, obeys me," she murmured. "Knight will not bite unless I order him to. Not like those beasts outside. Those are not mine."

Wayland's internal werewolf sighed with relief. He settled into the chair. "Whose are they?" he asked.

"I asked you a question first. You are the intruder. You must answer me."

He nodded, dumbfounded, aware his jaw was agape. "Um, well," he stumbled, "I traveled here from Ice Lake—"

"Ice Lake!" she erupted.

"Yes, well, I traveled up to Canada from the United States. Louisiana, to be exact."

"The deep south. Why so far? What is your business up here?"

Should he really blurt out his revenge plan? She'd obviously heard of the Tundra. Maybe he should eke out her feelings toward the Tundra first. But she beat him to the next question without waiting for his answer.

"What happened to your head?" She pointed to his makeshift turban bandage. "It's soaked through with blood, like your clothes."

"It's my ear. I injured it during a fight on my way here." He shrugged. "It won't kill me." That is, if he could wash and put salve on it soon. "Are you friendly with the Tundra?" he ventured. "My business has to do with their pack."

"The Tundra!" She exclaimed, snapping into an altogether different vein from a regal, staid woman. "Their pack is run by a sadistic thug!" Her pale skin flushed.

"Thorn?"

"Yes! Thorn! He's not who he says he is. He's a liar and a tyrant. Is that who you're doing business with?" Her tone was now infused with wariness.

"You could say I have *unfinished* business," Wayland replied. "About a year ago, he and his Tundra cohorts murdered my mate, Sabine, and my entire Leblanc pack. They almost killed me, too."

"That's terrible! You must be heartbroken."

"I went into a major depression. I couldn't sleep. I couldn't think straight. I was badly injured. The royal shifters' club down in Gloster, near the Red River, sent a member to Canada to collect me, what with all of my broken bones and ripped flesh, and to try to fix it all. They took me in, helped me find an apartment. I owe them." He chuckled darkly. "Hell, I still haven't unpacked. My place is full of cardboard boxes and dishes piled up on counters. A few weeks ago, I bombed up here in a camper I bought on impulse. It's the first major action I've taken. I'm here to get justice for myself, for the Leblanc slaughter."

"Justice, ha! That sounds excellent. It's the Tundra that locked me in here. Thorn comes every so often to terrorize me. I wonder even now if it's safe to get out!"

Wayland shook his head in worry. "We must be very careful, whatever we do."

"Yes. First, tell me the rest of your tale." Her voice softened. "I'm so sorry to hear of your troubles. I remember the Leblancs. They carried themselves with an admirable, measured strength."

"How did you know them? Did you live near Ice Lake?" Wayland had a million and more questions.

"I lived near Ice Lake for a time, many years ago. I was courted by Thorn's father, Jagger after Thorn's mother died."

"Oh! But you aren't Tundra?"

"I'm not Tundra. I'm not a Leblanc, and I'm not a Windrunner. Though I remember good times when many of the packs were friendly, or at least tolerated each other. I was an outsider, you might say." She eased into a mischievous grin. "I'm not a shifter though I'm not exactly a mortal either."

"My, god," Wayland mumbled. "What *are* you? Where are you from?"

"I am a high priestess—a witch descended from a woman who, in 1692, escaped a hanging at Salem. I used to live in Cape Cod."

Wayland nodded, trying to take in all the shocking new information.

"Thirty-five years ago, my fledgling coven journeyed to Canada with me to perform solstice rituals in the peace and beauty of the northern wilderness. On June twenty-first, I was sitting around the fire with my fellow witches when Jagger crept out of the blackberry bramble and stole my heart. He courted me all that summer and lured me away from my witch sisters with his brand of handsome poison. I had no idea what a philandering man he was, or how easily lies rolled off his tongue when he wanted something. During a waning moon, in that same bramble, we consummated our relationship. As the thunder cracked and rain poured down, my Stormy was conceived."

"Stormy!" Wayland exclaimed. "The Stormy who is Thorn's sister? The Stormy who is Tundra, who lives near Ice Lake?"

"His half-sister, yes. How do you know Stormy?"

"I've known her since childhood. I've run back into her since coming up to Canada. Wow, she's not full Tundra then. I've wondered—"

"No, she's not. You've fallen for my Stormy, is that it?" The woman, whose name he still didn't know, was beaming at him. Now he knew why she looked so familiar! Her face was a more world-wise version of Stormy. "My daughter is half witch, half Tundra."

"Holy fire, she has no idea! That explains so much!" Wayland started to laugh. The hound by the priestess's side raised his massive head and sniffed at Wayland, then, with a grunt, plunked it down.

"Yes, she was a spitfire, even at two!" The priestess let out a faint laugh, but her dark eyes dimmed again. "Your name? I didn't get your name?"

"Wayland Leblanc. Yours?"

"Eliza Hart." The witch sighed. "My beautiful, vibrant girl was taken from me at two, and I haven't seen her since. She doesn't even know I exist."

"That's dreadful! What happened?" Wayland asked.

"It turned out that Jagger quickly remarried after Thorn's

mother died, a wife he never told me about. She was a pure-bred Tundra, and they were obsessed with keeping their line pure." She sniffed in disgust. "They told me they would raise Stormy as their own. They stole the girl from my arms. They were nervous about anyone finding out she was half witch, but who knows whether she knew his newest wife wasn't her mom. Witches, even tiny ones, can sense things like that. Anyway, they feared if anyone knew Stormy's real origins, it would lessen their pack power, their impeccable reputation."

"Outrageous. So, he was heartless on top of being a cheater. My own father killed Jagger after he had the nerve to put the moves on my mother. The pain he caused went beyond even what I knew of him then."

"Yes. He was fixated on collecting women like trophies, but also on maintaining pure power at any cost. Glad to hear he eventually met his fate at your father's hands after I was imprisoned. Back then, I told Jagger and his new wife I would take little Stormy back to Cape Cod, live a quiet life with her, leave them alone." She gave Wayland a look of despair. "But that wasn't good enough for him. He grew determined not only to shut me up but to kill me."

"Oh, Eliza, I'm so sorry he put you through that. He was a sick, twisted brute." Wayland's gut churned. "What happened next?"

"Well, I had to make sure no one would kill me because then I'd never know if Stormy was safe. At that time, Thorn was a five-year-old terror, already a bully. I put a curse on him and his father." She chortled for the first time, lightening Wayland's spirit enough to dare ask what the curse was.

"Jagger could banish me if he was so compelled, but neither he nor his cronies could not kill me, for if they did, I warned Jagger my spell meant Thorn would automatically die too." She lifted her hands in glee. "You see? The perfect spell! Kill me, kill Thorn; spare me, and spare Thorn." She ran her hand along the chair's armrest. "Perfect...with one exception."

"What's that?" Wayland was hooked by Eliza's brilliant mind. Like her daughter, she took no bullcrap and her real-life saga had more dramatic turns than any witchy Tarot reading or dark Grimm's tale.

"Jagger found out about my special magic. You see, after he took my daughter from me, I threw my spirit into any living creature near her—the cats, a mouse, a baby rabbit—so I could talk to her and soothe her if she was scared and crying. She especially loved the butterflies called Silvery Blues."

"Blue butterflies! Those are Stormy's familiars!"

"Is that so! How wonderful." Eliza paused to take this news in then continued. "So, I would talk to Stormy this way. It was a blessing I could still reach her. Then, Jagger caught me, embodied in a kitten, telling Stormy a nursery rhyme. It must've looked strange, a fuzzy kitten meowing rhymes but Stormy had drawn close to it and was giggling. Jagger knew my voice. He was livid. He kicked that poor kitten away from my child and she started wailing." Eliza narrowed her eyes, glaring as if Jagger was there right in front of her in that underground lair. "He also found out that metal prevented me from my astral travels, because when his henchmen locked me in the Tundra prison lined with metal, I couldn't spirit travel." She gestured around her living quarters. "Thus, this house is also encased in metal, to ensure I never communicate with Stormy, or anyone."

"That is going to change," Wayland insisted. "I'm preparing for an epic battle against the Tundra. As I said, they need payback for the mass slaughter of the Leblancs. I will see to it that Thorn, his sidekick Ransom, and the Tundra involved get punished." He and Eliza locked eyes, and an electric current of camaraderie and determination ran from one to the other.

* * *

THEY FIGURED OUT A PLAN. It would be unsafe for Eliza to do any astral traveling at all. They would have to leave quietly. They would also have to put a replica of Eliza in her bed, lock the metal prison, and get past the guard dogs without them howling and attacking. Wayland would be unable to house Eliza in his minicamper. She would have to hunker down in a safe house, or somewhere so totally unexpected that the Tundra would never suspect and come snooping.

The idea floated in almost as a joke, but then it seemed perfect in the same way that Stormy had explained about the genius location of the Tundra's new digs: right in your face, reverse psychology.

"I know of a trendy new hotel for humans that all the locals, including the Tundra, hate," he explained to Eliza, over a tasty meal she'd prepared of roast bison and fern fronds and washed down with cranberry ale. "You can check in there under an alias but..." He eyed her crimson gown. "You'd have to wear something less flashy."

"Oh, I'll find an old ski jacket and leggings in my closet, maybe a big wool hat to gather up my hair," she assured him. "Like the ale?" He nodded. "The Tundra do keep me in gourmet food and drink. They airdrop the food once a month. It's the least they can do." They both got a cynical laugh out of this. She leaned over to pet Knight and her expression changed. "It will be sad to leave Knight, but what else can I do? Knight?" He gazed soulfully up into her eyes and Wayland could swear they engaged in a silent conversation. Knight licked her hand and gave a friendly yip. "He tells me he'll stay to guard this place until I can get him. He says he'll be the pack leader."

"To those attack dogs? Won't they slash his neck?"

"No, Knight and I have a plan." Her dark eyes gleamed with mischief. "A tiny bit of magic won't hurt once I open the door to the yard, will it?"

"I guess not."

"Then, it's settled!" Knight plunked his head on Eliza's foot. She didn't seem to mind. When she was done eating, she rested her elbows on the table and put her head in her hands. "Wayland, please tell me more about Stormy," she pleaded. "Oh, I can't wait to see my little girl."

"Now, she's a beautiful twenty-something-year-old woman," he remarked, thinking the same thing. He couldn't wait to wrap Stormy in his arms. He couldn't wait for her to know she had a mother who loved her, had always loved her, and that she had options now. "For one thing, Stormy has the same talent as you!" he said. "She also astral travels. We got to know each other again through her embodying my camp neighbor, Jacey, when it was too dangerous for us to visit otherwise." He laughed. "It's a handy skill."

"I'll bet. What does she look like now?"

"She's tall, like you. She has long black hair, all the way down her back, like you. She has your regal nose and cheekbones."

Eliza beamed at hearing this. "Oh, I can't wait to hug my daughter." She rose to clear the dishes, but Wayland stopped her. Let me do that. It's the least I can do for you."

"I won't argue. But I insist you take a hot bath and clean off that dried blood," Eliza said. "If we walk into that fancy hotel with you looking like a wounded warrior, we'll turn heads no matter if I'm wearing a boring jacket and pants or not. I can wash your bloody clothes and dry them by the fire. There's an oversized spare robe in the closet."

"Thanks. Are you sure you can climb down the trail? It's quite steep and slippery."

"Not a problem. I have boots with snow studs." She fetched them from her closet and held them up. They looked like old hobnail boots. Wayland was impressed with her bravado. "Will you be ready to leave in the morning, or do you need more time?"

"Ready at dawn! I can hardly wait!" Eliza said, and set off to run him a hot bath while he scrubbed the dishes.

CHAPTER 14

 ayland

Eliza made a lookalike body out of towels and old clothes on her bed and covered the form with a quilt. She put her small house back in order and packed lightly, though she did insist on carrying her staff.

Wayland winced. "You sure you need that? It's unwieldy. It won't fit in your pack."

"No, but I can stick it in my boots. I won't do much magic, but I'll need it for the dogs. You don't want them to bite your other ear off or eat your legs for breakfast, do you?"

"No." He described the sleeping pill venison wraps he'd fed them but said he had used up all his meds. Eliza claimed she had a spell for that, but he had his doubts.

The instant they cracked the door just an inch, fifteen slavering, snarling, part Mastiffs, part Dobermans, part freaking Hellhounds charged the door. Knight stood steady and stuck his nose out to sniff the air. Wayland's heart was up in his throat as Eliza raised her staff and chanted,

"Angry, biting beasts of Winter Crow,
Become friendly and docile. Play in the snow.
Follow Knight's every command,
His barks I ask you to understand.
Protect this compound. Do obey,
I will leave food and water once a day."

She waved the staff around and made a clicking sound with her tongue. With that, the dogs stopped smashing their limbs against the door, Knight bound outside and trotted off contentedly, greeting one hound after another like a furry social director.

Wayland whistled through his teeth. "You don't mess around!"

Eliza opened the door wider. "My magic is powerful when I choose to use it. Only metal can stop it."

They stepped into the snow. "Precious blessings!" she exclaimed, looking up in the sky and all around. "I haven't seen the light of day in years! The snow is beautiful!"

"You must be overwhelmed." Wayland zipped his coat up to his chin and eyed the dogs. "Could your magic fix that lock and get rid of the burn marks on the entryway? If we leave it bombed out, it will be a dead giveaway the next time the Tundra drop food here."

"I can try." Eliza waved her staff again and mumbled something under her breath, and the burned, twisted metal knit itself back together. She seemed as surprised as Wayland, running her hand over the newly smooth surface. "Funny, I can't do my magic *inside* the metal box, but I can fix the metal prison when I'm *outside* of it. Who knows why?"

"Curious," Wayland replied, weaving around the large dogs, chasing each other's tails. He couldn't escape from them fast enough. His ear was damaged from the Tundra, not the beasts, but he couldn't afford to lose another limb and he didn't trust them to stay friendly. Last night, Eliza had made a valiant effort to sew his old ear back on, but it was like a dried apple, leathery and curled in on itself in his collection jar. Plus, her magic didn't work inside the prison. Instead, she stitched the mangled flesh where his ear once was.

CHAPTER 15

 tormy

THORN TRIED to prove how nice he was by bringing her a basket of chocolates, which she had always devoured in one sitting. She couldn't help but nibble greedily on the corner of one bar. It was infused with rum and seeded with raisins. Holy Moonfire! The flavor burst like a shooting star on her tongue.

"I made it myself," Thorn said proudly. She believed him. He always was a talented cook, making crusty sourdough breads and zesty plum chutney to flavor meats. He tried to talk to her, reason with her. Promise her things. "You can have the pick of the Tundra alphas to marry. I mean, you're a virtual Tundra queen, Stormy. You're old enough to settle down. How about choosing Ransom? He's handsome, and smart, and would love to help make you a big family of cute little cubs. He's always had a crush on you, Stormy."

"Ugh. Ransom is too obsessed with fighting and sucking

113

up to you. I'm not the least attracted to him." Thorn grimaced, clearly taking issue with her 'sucking up' dig. But she saw him work to relax his gritted teeth and move on.

"Then what about Stark, my best scout?" he suggested. "He's fast, and protective. He'd always keep you safe. Guard your young. And he's pure Tundra, royal Tundra going back generations."

"Stark's a decent guy. But I have zero interest in him. I don't care about purebred lineage up the wazoo."

"You should. You're pure Tundra," Thorn insisted, his eyes taking on the maniacal glitter that happened when he spoke of pack virtue. It turned her off so hard, though she wasn't sure why. When she was younger, he could whip up in her a similar passion for pure bloodlines, a case for their superiority. But lately? The haughty lineage thing didn't even make sense to her anymore. Maybe she could see mating with an outsider just to make him squirm. Well, not just to make him squirm, and not any outsider. *Maybe a very special one...*

"By the way, Thorn, I don't need protecting!"

"Oh, really?" He rolled his eyes. "You'll thank me at some point that I'm protecting you from yourself!" With that, he stomped out and locked the cell.

Two days later, when he brought her an entire wild boar filled with oyster and walnut stuffing, she drew the line. "What do you think you're trying to accomplish with all the feasts?" she asked him.

"Can't I be nice to my sister? Is that a crime?" he asked, with a dimpled grin that was almost a leer.

"Let me out of this metal box! That would be super nice," she retorted.

"Look, I can't do that quite yet. I will though." He held out the boar on its gleaming silver platter, garnished with fresh parsley. It smelled so amazing her mouth watered.

She folded her arms stubbornly across her chest. "I'm on a hunger strike until you set me free," she announced. With a fierce howl, she high kicked the roast boar off its fancy platter for dramatic effect. It flew across the cell and *thwunked* onto the concrete floor, splattering meat juice on their ankles.

"You ungrateful wench!" shouted Thorn, giving it his own kick, making the stuffing explode everywhere. "Starve then. See if I care!" His fists were balled into rocky little boulders, which she knew meant he was tempted to land a vicious uppercut to her chin. He'd done that once when she was eight, and she'd had to go to the hospital for eleven stitches. "Where's Wayland?" he asked. "Tell me the truth. Don't fucking lie to me again!"

"He went back to Louisiana, I told you."

"That's bullshit!" His fists pumped reflexively.

"How do you know that it's bullshit?" Her heart pounded in her ears.

"I have my ways," he answered in a low snarl.

She wanted to beg him not to hurt Wayland. She wanted to spit on Thorn. She wanted to do a lot of things. But most of them would make matters worse. She could only hope the image of her getting thinner and weaker in front of his eyes as the days dragged on would tear open his cruel heart and let in a sliver of empathy.

She stumbled to her hard pallet and sprawled on it, facing away from him and holding back tears until she heard him secure the rusted padlock and his footsteps faded away.

Then, for the twentieth time, she tried to astral project. Nothing doing. So, she pictured Wayland holding her in his strong, welcoming arms, stroking her hair and comforting her until she stopped shaking.

CHAPTER 16

*W*ayland

BY SOME MIRACLE, he and Eliza made it down the craggy mountain and into the town of Gray Fiord. They didn't dare sleep at the Flintlock Inn, so they struggled on past it. At four in the morning, to the howl of the wind, they stumbled into a tight alcove of birch trees, thirty miles past Gray Fiord. The snow had finally stopped when they took their rest under a striking array of stars. By Wayland's estimation, they were more than halfway to the Snow Mountain Lodge.

He was incredulous that the witch Eliza had so much strength in her aging bones. He guessed she must have chanted a subtle spell for supernatural endurance. If she had, he wouldn't object, for he felt the heavy pressure of time bearing down on them both. He could've used a similar style spell, for his injured head throbbed where his ear once was, and his feet were raw and blistered. Eliza would not hear one word of complaint from him, though. Not after all she had suffered for so many years.

When they rose at dawn to continue their trek, he told tales to pass the time. He described the old candle-maker in Winter Crow. Eliza hadn't heard of her, but she expressed sympathy that the woman had sounded lonely, too. He described his pack club down at the Lazy Moon.

"I bet you'd like Louisiana," he said, "there are mysterious swamps and amazing creole food and other wise witches like you. Hell, they could use a high priestess to help guide them."

"You're too kind, Wayland. The heat, the food, the Lazy Moon, and the Wiccan community do sound delightful. I've been so solitary for many years. Thankfully, I had Knight." Her voice trailed off.

"Don't be sad, Eliza. We'll get him back."

"I hope so." She smiled valiantly and trudged on.

Long before they reached the Snow Mountain Lodge, she donned her down jacket and leggings and stuffed her long hair up into a knitted wool hat. He had given her a billfold of cash for food in case he had to be away from the hotel for a while.

So, in the late afternoon, when they finally walked along the hotel's plush gray carpet toward the vast welcome desk, under trendy ball-shaped lights in lollipop hues, they were prepared.

"A double room for the lady here, and a double for me. We are work colleagues," he explained out of sheer nerves, for who did this kind of explaining? On second thought, it couldn't hurt to have a backstory if they could keep it all straight.

"Names?" The clerk eyed them under blocky hipster frame glasses.

"Miss Elizabeth Twining," she said, with a polite smile.

"I'm Mr. Wharton," Wayland said. "William Wharton." It

was a blueblood kind of name that sounded beyond suspicion. "May we please be on the same floor, for convenience sake in our upcoming office meetings?" Wayland worked to keep his voice from wobbling.

"Certainly." The desk guy ran two cards through the magnetizer device, slipped them in paper sleeves and handed them over.

Even in the elevator, Wayland and Eliza said nothing, and glanced in opposite directions. There were lots of cameras around, and they felt it was best to act like they were distant coworkers.

It was twenty minutes later, once both were ensconced in their rooms, that they dared text each other. Earlier, Wayland had given Eliza a smart phone and walked her through the latest perks, since she hadn't held one for years.

Wayland: Glad we made it back in one piece. Keep a low profile.

Eliza: Thanks! Congrats to us!

Wayland: Might need to take care of business for the next few days. Will keep you posted.

* * *

WAYLAND WOKE A FEW HOURS LATER, sensing something was terribly amiss. The sky outside was still clear, though darkness had set in. He heard no yelling or other commotion in the hall. Maybe it was nerves, or simply exhaustion. He was out of sleeping pills, so God forbid his insomnia was kicking in again. He thought about switching on the TV for distraction. Instead, his eyes shifted to the right of the TV. He stared at a chic photo on the wall—skiers lined up on Snow Mountain in over-cheery gear—and growled at it under his breath. "Damned people taking over the wilds."

He wondered how Stormy was, and whether her brother

was making her life miserable. He finally had the evidence of Thorn's full brutality that he'd been seeking. Even before he'd rescued Stormy's mother and had the information that might change Stormy's mind, something had shifted for him. He now knew which beautiful, complex, sassy she-wolf he wanted to be with, who made his heart sing. His state of mind had changed gradually. But it switched, finally and completely, when he was soul-searching, alone in that room at the Flintlock Inn. When he called out her name not for sex, not to tease or joke around, but as a hymn from his innermost heart.

It would be Stormy's choice though—totally her choice. He hoped that it would be a clear choice when she found out how viciously she'd been duped. He hoped she felt as strongly as he did, because them being at odds emotionally was painful to imagine. He prayed it wasn't too late, that her heart hadn't hardened against him.

Another worry crept into Wayland's mind—in the forthcoming battle, if he was fated with the chance to kill Thorn, would that be a bridge too far for Stormy?

To see her brother die at my hands?

Sleep was impossible. He rose and changed into clean clothes, and padded out softly. He followed his wolf instincts like he did when in the forest, scenting and searching the invisible threads that pulled him. When he was safely past the hotel and into the woods, he changed to his wolf form— to run swiftly and fully utilize his sense of smell.

He skirted the Tundra field, where he knew they lay in their underground den, plotting his demise. His inner compass led him toward his old campsite, where his mini-camper was still parked. He'd paid for a full month when he registered, so he didn't have to worry about anyone impatiently poking around to claim the campsite space next.

When he drew close enough to track in the scent, he recoiled.

Tundra! The stink of rancid fisher cat blood!

Then, he heard a loud ruckus.

"Get off me, you creep!" Suze bellowed.

She was followed by Jacey, warning, "Fuck off or I'll put a curse on your ass!"

"Try it, witch! You don't scare me," someone roared.

Wayland peered through the foliage at Jacey, beginning to chant loudly in a foreign language. The Tundra responded by writhing and pitching onto the ground.

Wayland had seen enough. He unwound his whip from his belt loops and charged in, transforming to his full were-wolf at the same time. With a sharp howl, he cracked the whip over a Tundra shifter who was on top of Suze and had his pants half off. Over and over he whipped the Tundra's back and butt, which spurted deep rows of blood.

Yowling, the Tundra struggled to his feet and lurched forward, his legs still tangled in his lowered pants. Watching him tripping like a moronic clown on his clothes could've been funny in itself. But molesting a woman, even a badass witch, wasn't funny in the least. Wayland smacked the whip sideways at head level, splitting the Tundra's eyeballs in half. The Tundra fell, grabbing at his ruined eyes.

Next, Wayland leapt on Jacey's attacker and injected his long claws into the shifter's jugular. The intruder rolled over and groaned, bleeding out on the dirt. It wasn't lost on Wayland that Jacey had already turned the guy's legs into stone.

Suze stumbled up and dusted herself off. "At least the fucker was too drunk to get my pants off." Then she saw Wayland in his full werewolf form. "Holy crap! Who are you?"

"Oh, whoops. Don't mean to scare you even more. Let me, um, transform." He shifted back to wolf, then human.

"You're Wayland! Whoa, that's some impressive shit!" Suze marveled.

"So, you were that freaking wolf man we saw kill the bear a few weeks ago!" Jacey exclaimed. "Wow, you're ripped!"

They padded toward him. He reached out and held them both in a group hug. "Ladies, are you okay? I'm so, so sorry that the Tundra got to you in their search for me."

"Who are they?" asked Suze after they broke the hug. "And why do they want to harm you?"

Jacey spat on the shifter whose legs she'd turned to stone. "Whoever they are, they're despicable," she snapped, watching her spittle drip from his chin to his bloody shoulders.

"They are deadly rivals. They killed my whole pack a year ago. Look, I can explain more, later. I know of a safe house where you two can go for a few days if you want. There are beds and a hot shower. Food and a fellow witch."

"A fellow witch! I'm in," said Jacey.

"Me too," said Suze. "I can't wait to shower off the stink of that nasty shifter."

They packed a few things and left. Wayland figured the Tundra had probably rifled through his camper before they hit the neighboring site, but he would check it some other time.

CHAPTER 17

$\mathcal{W}$ ayland

AT SNOW MOUNTAIN LODGE, Wayland rented the witches another double suite, thinking they might as well be comfortable. Luckily, the desk guy was oblivious, and more interested in scrolling through his social media on his smart phone than scrutinizing the disheveled, upset ladies. Wayland promised to fill them in first thing in the morning. Everyone was way too fatigued and stressed to deal with more conversation. He bid them goodnight and this time, was able to sleep.

At dawn, he and the witches convened in Eliza's room. Wayland brought them hot coffee and muffins from the gourmet café in the hotel's lobby, and they sat in rows on the edges of the two beds.

Eliza had changed into dove gray leggings and a braided Swiss sweater. Her long white hair was swept into a bun.

Suze's blonde hair was freshly washed, and she wore a low-cut red sweater and jeans. Jacey had on black sweats and a purple jersey. Wayland had to admit, he got a momentary rise out of seeing her. After all, he was an alpha male and she was a tall, elegant woman who looked sexy in purple. But she reminded him of Stormy, and Stormy quickly filled his thoughts. God, he missed her. He was on a mission—war, justice, and hopefully, Stormy. He explained to Suze and Jacey who Eliza was, and they explained to Eliza how they knew him.

"It blows me away that you endured almost twenty-three years of lockup," Suze told Eliza. "I would've gone full out fruit loops in like, a month."

"It was hard. But I learned one can survive incredible hardships." Eliza visibly shivered. "It already seems like a lifetime ago. I'm ready to live. Ready to reconnect with my daughter. What brought you ladies up to Canada?"

"The solstice, the wilderness, and why not? We came from New Hampshire," said Jacey. "Where was your home…I mean, before all of the horror?"

"Not so far from yours. I lived in Massachusetts, on Cape Cod."

"Ah! Practically sister covens!" Suze declared, and the ladies did a round of high fives.

Wayland was pleased the three ladies were bonding over a few more descriptions of their towns and home covens.

When the topic came back to Stormy, Wayland felt compelled to again tell Jacey he was sorry Stormy went through her to get to him.

"I appreciate the sentiment, thanks," said Jacey. "But it wasn't your doing. Besides, I'm happy to help a girl out." She giggled and winked at Wayland. "And, hey, we had some hot moments."

These were smart, accomplished women. They should

know exactly what would transpire later today. Wayland detailed his war strategy with his allies, the coyote shifters.

"Can we help you?" Jacey asked. "You saw me turn that Tundra's legs to stone."

"That was way impressive," Wayland admitted.

"Yeah, we'll spell cast," Suze chimed in. "My sweetie, Red Claw, will be all for it. Together, we could kick some very serious ass. I mean, as serious as that ass-whipping you gave that Tundra pervert last night."

Wayland glanced at Eliza with a raised brow. "You promised up and down and sideways you wouldn't cast any spells to attract attention to your whereabouts."

"Right, it's not a bad idea though, Wayland," Eliza ventured, grinning at her newfound witch friends.

"But how can I protect you from the Tundra if, by some twist of fate, they discover where the Wiccan energy is coming from?" he asked her. "If anything happened to you, I'd never forgive myself, and Stormy would never get to meet you."

"It's a gamble," Eliza murmured. "But a worthy one. We three could be quite powerful together—with my astral traveling, Jacey's ability to turn flesh to stone, and Suze's…"

"My ability to swirl up magical clouds—to confuse and camouflage," Suze replied.

"Okay, you've all convinced me. So, hell, it's a go, and welcome to the battle! I've got to alert the coyote team. We need the edge that early morning provides." Wayland jumped up, downed the last of his coffee, and headed for the door. He turned, taking them all in, to remember them all in case everything went horribly, fatally wrong. Though he told himself it was only a random look. "I'll text you, Eliza. If I lose the phone or it's too dangerous, I'll get one of the coyote shifters to send you a vision shout-out. I think Bones knows how. This starts today—first by the

Tundra den, and later, near Ice Lake. At least that's our plan."

"Good. And I'll holler back through my astral voice," Eliza reassured him. "Put a critter in your pocket—a cricket, a dragonfly, any small live being. I'll talk through it."

He nodded, wondering what godforsaken creature he could find, and whether he had a secure pocket. He reached down to the front of his corduroy shirt. *Check.* Pockets with pearl snaps.

Suze and Jacey gave him the thumbs up, and he walked out.

* * *

WAYLAND WENT on a quick hunt for fresh kills. The feast would be for his coyote allies before the epic battle—a gift for endurance and loyalty. The forest seemed overhunted today, or maybe he was still too near the noisy Snow Mountain Lodge. Further in, along the creeks, he had better luck. He filled his pack with fat trout, two badgers, and a raccoon. He got even luckier and bagged a wild boar. He dragged the weighty motherlode to the coyote headquarters and before he even dropped it on the edge of the fire pit, Bones ran up to him with a troubled frown.

"My friend, I'm glad you're back. I have some difficult news…"

Dread, like snake toxin, spread through Wayland's veins. He'd just been hunting and his senses were already limbered up, quite acute. He envisioned Stormy pacing in a confined space. "Tell me!"

"I was in World's Edge the other day, and Ransom, Thorn's second in command was talking about Stormy— how Thorn had her locked in the old Tundra prison and—"

"Oh no! I should never have gone up north and left her

here to fend for herself." Wayland broke out in a sweat and his claws reflexively extended. "What are we waiting for? We have to get her out!" He gripped Bones's shoulders and shook them.

Bones patiently picked off his hands. "Come to your senses, brother. We have a war to fight. Knowing Thorn, he's moved her somewhere else, because he's paranoid and no doubt his scouts have found out the battle's about to begin."

Wayland struggled to keep his werewolf muscles, hair, and fangs from taking over his body and his mind. The rush of murderous adrenaline was drowning him. "He's going to kill her! He's—"

"Brother, we need to stay the course," Bones reminded him. "If anything, he'll use her as bait, a lure. He won't kill her. If he kills her, he has nothing."

Hearing Bones's sensible logic calmed Wayland long enough to ignore the hatred pumping through him and to use his higher brain. "You're right. Tell your guys to eat fast. Let's get to that Tundra den before those fuckers get up. I was going to give them fair warning, but all bets are off."

"That's the spirit!" Bones called to the other coyote shifters. They each grabbed a raw fish, hunk of bloody boar, or raccoon flank on their way to gear up with whips, leather vests and stashes of venison jerky to keep their energy zooming.

Red Claw appeared, his hair in braids and surrounded by an entire headdress of glossy raven feathers and a whip slung around his waist. He saluted Wayland.

Wayland paused his frenzy long enough to fully admire the ragtag coyote warriors and give them a rousing huzzah. And to pick up a grasshopper and place it gingerly in his pocket, then snap it shut without squashing the thing.

Then, the warriors streaked through the forest and toward the Tundra den to surprise all hell out of them.

* * *

WAYLAND AND BONES led the way into the underground den like a fleet of thirsty vampire bats out for blood. It was just where Stormy said it would be—the opening was behind a boulder on the side of the Tundra training field.

The coyotes shifted to pumped up steroidal freaks—growing nearly a foot in height, sprouting shaggy, matted hair the color of stale caramel, and their fangs and jagged claws protruding. Wayland also expanded into his full were-wolf with glittering amber eyes, jet-black hair springing from every part of him, a chest like a gorilla's, and deadly, razor-sharp, claws and fangs.

As they hoped, the Tundra shifters were still lounging in bed, and the ragtag warriors were able to slaughter half a dozen before the Tundra alphas sprang to action. The she-wolves grabbed their cubs and fled, screeching and howling, out of a back tunnel.

Wayland ran down twisty underpasses in search of Thorn or Ransom. If he could quickly chop off the dual snakeheads of leadership, he could hasten the end of the battle with fewer lives lost.

No such luck. From his side eye, he saw a movement and a flash of metal. He veered just in time to avoid a Tundra shifter's knife. Instead, the blade sank into the flank of a coyote shifter, who howled in pain. Wayland attacked the Tundra's jugular, slashing the neck so thoroughly the shifter's head wagged on hunks of neck, blood gushing onto the floor.

He was helping the coyote ally up when a pair of Tundra fighters charged him. Wayland had no time to unwind his whip or plan a method of attack. One jumped on his back and sank his fangs into Wayland's shoulder. Another forced his arm backward into a torturous position. Wayland wriggled, madly trying to twist from the shifter's arm pin and out of the other shifter's grip on his back.

Red Claw appeared, flying raven feathers framing his ruddy face. He emitted the coyotes' war whoop, a piercing *hoo-yowl*, then spun the whip in a wicked-fast curve. The cord wound around the Tundra's neck and Red Claw yanked the shifter off Wayland's back. Wayland then bucked and knocked off the guy pinning his arm. He snatched the first Tundra's knife from his belt and sank it deep into his chest while the guy was still struggling to free his neck of Red Claw's whip. Red Claw was on to the next Tundra warrior, when a third one somersaulted up to him and bashed him in the jaw with his colossal clawed feet.

Red Claw groaned, and crashed hard on his back. Wayland and another coyote who had run into the lair tackled the somersaulting Tundra and bashed his meaty head onto a rock protruding from the tunnel floor. He helped Red Claw up.

After that, it was utter madness, the tunnel filling with howling Tundra and coyote warriors screeching *hoo yowls* and *yip yip howls* to help locate allies. Someone had kicked out the lanterns, so only by the glow of Wayland's own eyes, and those of the other shifters, was he able to see anything at all. He could track and slay the Tundra by their reek of fisher cat and sour dirt. He went on a vicious rampage, stepping over Tundra bodies, which smelled of cooling blood, while scenting out live, breathing ones to continue the kill.

The battle spilled out along every Tundra chamber, and Wayland saw to his horror that many coyotes had met their Maker—carved up with Tundra blades, sprawled in contorted positions, and arms and flanks bent backward like branches after a hurricane, sometimes severed completely.

Thankfully, there was no sign of Bones and Red Claw, but also no sign of Thorn or Ransom. What about Stormy?

Wayland took a moment to breathe and analyze the scents in the tunnels. No whiff of blue phlox. She must still be far from here. With another long inhale, it was clear all the tunnels were filled with dead. The living had gone to the next battlefield.

Ice Lake.

That was where the old Tundra den was, and their underground prison where Stormy had been—maybe still was. "Bones!" Wayland yelled, then, "Red Claw!"

In answer, he heard a faint *yip-yip-howl*, and another *yip-yip-howl*. This was the coyotes' signal to identify their locations. Wayland made his way out of the den and into the blinding light. *Yip-yip-howl* was louder this time.

Wayland ran toward the calls, across the field strewn with Tundra and coyote corpses, and into the dense woods.

About three minutes in, he heard the crackle of sticks breaking, and spun around just in time to see a Tundra alpha, knife raised, somersault toward him. The blade sank into Wayland's right arm, just under his shoulder. He winced and grabbed the shifter, tumbling into the underbrush. There was a mad struggle for supremacy, and then a sharp cracking of a whip. The Tundra fell off him, tongue wagging sideways from his muzzle.

Bones rolled up his whip, ran over and helped Wayland to his feet. He took a scarf and the hooch from his pocket, poured some on Wayland's wound, then twisted and knotted the scarf firmly around that arm.

"Man, thanks, I wasn't sure I was—"

"Don't even say it. Don't even *think* it," Bones implored. He helped Wayland to a rock where he could sit and catch his breath. They both took a swig of hooch.

"Any visioning pictures?" Wayland asked Bones. "I've heard nothing from Eliza yet. I figure Thorn and Ransom are long gone from that den we were in, if they were there at all.

When I left it, there were no more live Tundra…or coyote shifters."

Bones scrunched up his eyes, which accentuated his laugh lines—deeply earned wrinkles of a life well-lived. "I'm getting something from Red Claw. He's over by Ice Lake. They're fighting over there. Says he saw Ransom but not Thorn."

Wayland leapt up. "Let's get over there."

"You don't want to take one more minute to get your strength back? It's gonna be a very long day."

"I'm good. Thanks, bro." Wayland gave Bones a friendly clap on the back. "I owe you."

"Buy me a shot of whiskey at World's Edge after we win this war," he quipped. They shifted to their slimmer, sleeker wolf and coyote selves to streak through the woods at warp speed.

CHAPTER 18

 tormy

W<small>HEN</small> T<small>HORN CAME</small> to rouse her, Stormy was weak from hunger. For three days she had only allowed herself water; she'd eaten no food at all.

Thorn had tried his best to tempt her with iced currant cake, roast lamb with mint he'd gathered in the forest, an endless array of handmade chocolates on platters with lace doilies, and Gooseberry wines. He left the treats there to tempt her, lined up on a long table he'd installed in the prison.

"Where are you taking me?" she asked him. "Are you setting me free?"

He sniggered in response. "I told you. I have to protect you from yourself."

She eyed his getup, a paramilitary body shield with metal plates she'd never seen him wear. Chills ran through her famished body. "Why do you have that armor on?"

"Wouldn't you like to know?" His laugh was maniacal.

"Let me go or I'll starve myself. You want a dead sister?"

"I know you snuck something down your gullet when I wasn't looking—a piece of chocolate or a slice of lamb. It's not like you to deny yourself."

"You don't think I'm serious?" He didn't answer, only pulled harder on her arm.

During the last few days, Thorn had been doting and conversational. He'd sat at the table while she lay on the pallet, and relayed stories of when they were little—of dressing in costume and putting on plays, of helping her set up tea parties with her dolls. Clearly, he was trying to make her nostalgic. He fawned over her, saying what a beautiful sister she was, how she could rule over Ice Lake and Snow Mountain. Hell, over the whole province if she wanted to! "With the right shifter by your side," he reminded her. "If not Ransom or Stark, there's always Axel, who is almost as good at cooking as me. He'd keep you in scones and homemade sherbets."

She had rolled around to face him, sitting up with effort. "Forget it, Thorn," she snapped. "I'm not interested in your cohorts, even if they're five-star chefs."

"Only rival shifters, is that it?" His fists balled in knots again, his face reddened with fury. These days, it took less and less to rile him to scary levels.

She had left the food alone, but now, after he cuffed her and dragged her roughly from the cell, she reached out and batted away as many delicacies as she could, smashing the wine and the platter of chocolates to the floor. Glass shattered everywhere. A few shards landed in her leg, but she didn't care.

As he pulled her along the prison hall, Thorn repeated his tired old lines about her choosing a Tundra alpha for a mate, and how there was still time to change her mind. If she did, she would be a pampered Tundra elite for the rest of her days.

Not now, not ever. My brother is such a lost, pathetic cause.

To him, she shouted, "I'll pick a rival shifter! The more powerful, the better!"

He tied a blindfold over her eyes, clipped a chain to her cuffs, yanked her outside, and threw her in the double-lined metal ATV he'd brought her here in, making sure she was chained inside it. He drove off madly, grinding the motor.

Shit. She still had no way to astral travel to Wayland's side. Where on earth was he now? She had lost the thread of connection and it was killing her more surely than the lack of food.

CHAPTER 19

Wayland

ICE LAKE! Wayland and Bones broke through the forest enough to glimpse the glittering waters that Wayland used to call his home base. Transforming back to their steroidal werewolf shapes, they charged forward into the action, taking on three Tundra shifters at a time. The arm bandage Bones had wrapped for Wayland had staunched the bleeding, but the force of new battle broke the wound open again.

Wayland and Bones worked as a team—one with the whip, and the other charging and leaping with fangs sunk into the weakest parts of flesh and tearing it open.

Around the lake, the coyotes were busy playing a vicious round of Whack-a-Mole, crouching in their hidey-holes only to pop up suddenly with howls and whips cracked around Tundra ankles, tripping them. Tundra alphas dropped their knives and careened into the pits to meet their fate.

Wayland and Bones looked sorrowfully on the dozen

coyote corpses strewn on the banks by the lake. They were relieved not to see Red Claw, but were worried for the coyote shifter's welfare. They searched the vista for Thorn's meaty head, heavy brow and torso, and perpetual glower.

"Where's the fucker?" Bones whispered. "What's his plan?"

"Must be to hide in a bunker like a coward," snarled Wayland.

Out of Wayland's shirt pocket, Eliza's disembodied voice rang out. It startled both alphas until Wayland remembered the grasshopper and whispered to Bones that he'd explain it all soon. Amazingly, he hadn't crushed the thing. Forget about smart phones, Eliza had it covered with critter-circuits!

"What can we do?" she squeaked through the grasshopper's mandible.

"Locate Thorn," he growled back.

"Thorn is not on my radar. Anyone else?"

"Stormy?"

"No astral signal at all. Sorry."

"Ransom then, Thorn's right-hand man."

"Hold on," the grasshopper cheeped. "A shifter just yelled for Ransom, over by your old Leblanc den, south of where you stand."

"Thanks! Roger that!" Wayland felt silly using flight lingo, but what the hell?"

He and Bones had been headed toward the old Tundra den on the lake's north side, but quickly switched course.

A Tundra wolf in a leather mask spotted Wayland and howled for his soldiers to follow. A formation of Tundra pivoted and gave chase.

Shit! Time's running out, I've got to finish this!

Wayland ran faster. Bones matched his every step.

"Witches—Is Suze there?" Wayland panted frantically into his pocket. "Suze—Tundras at the lake are chasing us!"

In moments, Wayland heard Tundra coughing behind him and stole a look over his shoulder. Dense clouds of purple dust twisted up from the earth like mini tornados. The cluster of Tundra shifters choked and wheezed through the blinding haze. They toiled forward, but much slower.

Suze's miraculous magic bought Bones and Wayland the precious seconds they needed to round the south end of the lake. There they spotted Ransom.

The slim Tundra alpha, surrounded by his flunkies, had a leather bomber hat over his pure white head of hair. In his werewolf form, his already bulky shoulders had blown up to strange balloon shapes. Even at a distance, Wayland spotted the howling wolf tattoo on the alpha's hairless chest peeking out from his leather vest.

What kind of narcissistic A-hole shaves his chest to show off a tat? I should've slaughtered Ransom in our fight at World's Edge the day I arrived. But now...

Wayland snarled, "For the kill."

"*Hoo yowl!*" Bones rumbled, and then nodded to a place behind Ransom. "Look!"

Red Claw, in his feather headdress, was creeping toward Ransom. He emitted a sudden, soulful *wail-yowl-woo* and dozens of coyote shifters mirrored the call *wail-yowl-woo* from their various trenches. This was the signal to drive the Tundra into Ice Lake. Ransom's guards spun and went after Red Claw. Other coyote shifters, anticipating this, surrounded Ransom's henchmen and brutally tackled them.

Ransom scurried away from the brawl, and seemed temporarily stunned at all the coyote shifters leaping from trenches around the lake. The coyotes charged toward the lake, confronting Tundras and forcing them to the water.

Hoo yowl! Hoo Yowl!

"Over here!"

"Watch out!"

"Behind you!"

Hoo yowl!

Wayland and Bones, too, took an instant to observe their war strategy play out. Wayland worried the battle was too evenly matched. On the muddy banks, Tundra stabbed coyote shifters or high jumped onto their shaggy backs and viciously tore at the coyotes until muscle and bone were exposed. Still, many coyote shifters managed to whip or kick away the Tundra's knives, trap them in a tightening cordon and force them into deeper waters. Soon, the lake was roiling with fighting swimmers and it was hard to see who was who. The Tundra shifters were almost as strong swimmers as the coyotes, so unless the coyotes could outnumber them, neither side would gain the edge.

Wayland kept a sharp eye on Ransom's whereabouts as he and Bones stalked closer along the lake's muddy edge. Ransom saw them, and advanced with two of his henchmen. "Eliza!" Wayland growled. "Alert Jacey to do her magic on the Tundra in Ice Lake. And Eliza?"

"Yes?" cheeped the grasshopper.

"Throw your voice all over the place. Make it sound like me, like Bones, like any shifter who isn't Tundra. Confuse the holy hell out of them. Any sense of Stormy yet?"

"No, but if she's out, I'll know. Good luck!"

"Thanks. I'll be in the water. I'm letting this grasshopper go." He heard a loud chirp from the insect's mandible as he tossed it into the bramble.

Wayland and Bones charged Ransom, now a couple of yards away. Ransom leapt at them, brandishing a curved saber he drew from a hidden pocket on his pants leg. Bones was closest, and before Wayland could intervene, Ransom plunged the saber between Bones' ribs. Bones, with

Ransom still on him, groaned and slid into the muddy bank.

"Hang on," Wayland called to Bones. Ransom clambered up. Wayland dug his claws into either side of Ransom's neck, about to slit the Tundra's throat, when Ransom's men charged, trying to pull Wayland off and sink their blades in him.

"Behind you! Watch out!" yelled Ransom's disembodied voice from at least two locations.

Eliza!

Ransom's henchmen turned their heads in confusion, long enough for Wayland to kick them each in the crotch so brutally they fell, unconscious. Ransom, groaning loudly and clutching his bloody neck, staggered to his feet again. He grabbed Bones and gave him a feeble push into the lake. Bones's legs dipped into the water, while his arms and head stuck firmly to the mud bank. Wayland would come for his friend soon. But first, he needed to end it with Ransom. He grabbed Ransom by the back of his wide belt, lifting him up in a murderous rush of adrenalin.

"Where is Thorn, you lackey? Tell me where!" There was no answer from Ransom. Wayland shook him hard, causing blood to pour from the shifter's slashed neck. "Where's Stormy? Huh?" Wayland shouted, leaning close enough to stare right into the dying Tundra's crystalline eyes. When Ransom stayed silent, Wayland snarled, "Time's run out, you vile creep!" He let out a monstrous roar and ripped Ransom's head clear off, hurling it into Ice Lake. "Take that for hurting Bones!" He watched Ransom's bomber hat float off, and his white mop of hair drift then slowly sink.

On Ice Lake, purple mists spiraled up, so many magic tornadoes, and voices sprang out all over the water like thousands of disembodied frogs. "Here!" "No, here!" "He's about to dunk you!"

Hoo yowl! Yip! Yip!

Heads bobbed in mass confusion and the waters churned with blood.

Tundra pushed back against coyote shifters, frantically treading water, when the lake unexpectedly started bubbling. Tundra screamed in agony, "My legs!" "I'm sinking!" "I can't feel my damn legs!" "They've fucking turned them to stone!"

Wayland had no time to gloat over Jacey's wondrous magic. Nor did he have time to move Bones from where he lay. Wayland could only pray the coyote shifter would be safe for now—the Tundra would take him for dead.

Wayland's attention was drawn to Red Claw's urgent shouts from the north side of the lake. "Boss! Over here, boss!" A grinding racket of what sounded like a military tank followed Red Claw's calls. Holy fire! Wayland spotted Red Claw in a tree, pointing down to a soldier in full paramilitary gear, stepping out of a steel-plated ATV. He saw the fleshy, glowering face of Thorn. In Thorn's clutches was a rail-thin, gray-faced Stormy with Thorn's knife at her neck.

CHAPTER 20

*S*tormy

THE SUN almost blinded her when Thorn removed her mask. She was still cuffed so running was not an option.

Not yet.

She blinked and inhaled.

Forest, pine, a cold, fresh body of water. Ice Lake!

Thorn held tight to the chain attached to her handcuffs and pressed his blade into her neck enough to warn her not to flinch or pull away.

She blinked again, her sight adjusting, and what she saw across the lake had her heart pounding with fear and a faint hope.

Wayland!

He was in full werewolf form—his pumped-up body covered with black fur, hulking shoulders, and claws as long and sharp as steak knives. But she knew him by his eyes, now tinged with amber, yet still handsome and lively.

He saw her, too. She could tell by the way he froze mid-movement, his eyes glued to her. His male beauty was astounding, yet painful because it could be snuffed out in an instant. His mouth fell open. She could almost hear him gasp.

Her brother's voice thundered out, bruising her inner ears. But she dared not recoil. "Okay, Leblanc!" he yelled. "You have a choice. I kill her now, or you surrender, and she lives but you never see her again."

"False choice!" Wayland roared back. "My fighters have already won against your Tundra, so no surrender's necessary. Your shifters lay lifeless on your own battlefield, and now they've sunk in Ice Lake with their legs turned to stone." Almost in response, waves on the uneasy lake could be heard lashing the banks. There were so many silent dead —in the water and in the mud. Stormy heard just a handful of moans.

Thorn snorted. "You needed your witch's magic to quell my warriors? You cheat!"

"Cheat? That's a laugh. Where were you while your Tundra warriors fought? Cowering in your little bunker! Your shifters used knives, not claws. We killed most of your shifters with our own power, maybe a few whips—to whip you into shape." Wayland's rough chuckle filled Stormy with conflicting emotions—a memory of holding each other, warm and safe in his camper, and a sinking dread that Wayland's taunts would tip her deranged brother into a killing spree that no one would escape. If he had paramilitary gear, he might also have an arsenal of bombs. If Thorn felt he'd already lost, he might burn the whole proverbial village down with him.

"Cowering?" Thorn replied. "Here I am! And I have the treasure you seek but will never win." He pulled Stormy by her hair to show her off. Her scalp burned. Every fiber in her longed to hurt him. "So, give me a reason to keep her alive.

Leave Canada now and never return. That would be a start, but I'd need more."

"No deals, no trades. Your sister can make up her own mind. Is using force the only way you can keep her loyal?" Wayland shook his head as he ventured forward and slowly closed the gap between him and where she stood with her brother. Her heartbeats matched his steps, as if they were drawing Wayland closer.

"She's been loyal to the Tundra pack," Thorn insisted. "I've treated her well over the years." Stormy wanted to scream, to spit in Thorn's face, but the knife still grazed her neck.

"Grabbing her by her hair and cuffing her doesn't strike me as great treatment," Wayland scoffed as he marched forward. "Give *her* the choice. Stormy?"

"Leblanc, come any closer and it won't end well." Thorn pressed the blade hard to her jugular. "Stormy, same goes for you. Talk to him and you're a goner."

She should be terrified. Thorn was always quick to anger, full of jealousy, but now? He had completely lost his shit. She was dizzy from hunger and exhaustion. Wayland was asking her to say what she wanted while Thorn still had her cuffed. Yet, a tiny inner peace wafted through her. No, a *presence*. Not Wayland's, but a female essence. It was warm, containing emotional energy, and like dipping into summer creek waters. She strained to identify it, but it passed.

"Talk about cheating," Wayland derided, "your tanks and body armor are not the alpha wolf way. Those are human war toys. My help from witches is much more suited to us shifters. No matter what you, Stormy, or I decide, a dark fate stalks you. It will follow you like the devil and lead you straight to hell."

Stormy heard Thorn's sharp intake of breath at Wayland's dire prediction. She knew her brother was superstitious. But why was Wayland goading Thorn? Did he have a secret strategy, or was he so beside himself with rage he was out of control? He wasn't the type. Had something changed?

"It was fun slaughtering your Leblanc pack," Thorn retorted. "I would do it again. You were practically dead when we went after your precious Sabine—"

Wayland lifted his head, roaring and foaming at the mouth like a rabid wolf. Stormy could only imagine the intensity of his pain. He followed this with a piercing howl, but after a moment he held his ground and went on.

"You think you're so pure, don't you?" he snapped. "Now that the Leblancs are out of your way, you assume your lily-white Tundra pack can rule the world." Stormy could hear a coyote shifter in the woods snorting at this. Wayland continued. "I know you've told your sister how she's a purebred Tundra and only a purebred Tundra wolf would be good enough to be her mate, but I have news for you, Thorn!"

Stormy's ears pricked. Wayland was certainly an alpha brimming with surprises. He'd better get on with it, though, before Thorn killed her or himself, or blew up the whole darn territory.

That warm breezy energy wrapped around her again. Yes, it was exactly like a hug. It lifted her up with a buoyant inner strength, though she had no clue how or why.

Wayland, still advancing, wagged his hand at Thorn. "You've been lying to your precious sister ever since she was two years old!"

"About what?" Stormy rasped.

"Quiet!" Thorn tightened his grip on her hair and drew his blade across the surface of her neck. "Just a preview of what I can do." Warm liquid trickled down her collarbone. "Leblanc, you're the dishonest one!" he shouted.

"I tell the truth and you know it!" howled Wayland. "Stormy's only half Tundra!"

"What?" Stormy cried, struggling to turn and look up at Thorn.

Her brother shook his head as he stared down at her. "No! Leblanc is a deceitful, two-faced monster. I told you he was bad news!"

"Stormy, your mother still lives!" yelled Wayland. "Your brother and his henchmen have held her prisoner for over twenty years. I can prove it."

Stormy's heart exploded with a long-repressed hope. She had to speak out, no matter the cost. "Tell me the truth, Thorn, no more bull!" she squeaked, the knife cramping her airflow. "What's he talking about?" Thorn just shook his head.

A stronger wave of cosmic energy flowed through her, and a soft, insistent voice was in her head.

Believe Wayland. I live.

"Where are you?" Stormy whispered under her breath.

"I'm here," said Thorn.

Not you, you murderous bastard, said a voice in her head. Not hers, then whose?

Wayland was only a canoe's length from them. She heard his heavy breaths and sensed his intense need to deliver her the facts. "Your mother is a high priestess; a witch who can astral travel," Wayland bellowed. "Like you, Stormy—you magnificent wolf-witch!"

Stormy's heart melted and burned with Wayland's words. "Blessed goddess! Is it real?" she whispered. A deep well of forgotten experience rushed in—her mother rocking her and singing, teaching her to walk, and giggling at her mother reciting nursery rhymes to her through a kitten, its whiskers twitching, its pink tongue flicking.

My mother has the same unique talent I do.

She felt Thorn's grip on her hair loosen in his utter shock.

Gentle currents of energy rocked her like the waves on

Ice Lake before it rained. Something epic was underway—the ground shifting underfoot. She sensed a shifter moving behind her but didn't let on.

She could see from Wayland's eyes he saw it too, but he didn't move his head to acknowledge it.

Suddenly, a coyote *hoo yowled* behind her and her brother. More *hoo yowls* rang out, and Thorn's ATV motor revved and screeched away from the lake, Red Claw's raven feathers streaming from the open window.

Thorn whirled around. "You filthy coyote bastard!" he howled. The ATV sent up broken twigs as it disappeared into the forest.

No more getaway car for Thorn, Stormy thought with a vengeful glee.

When Thorn spun to see what was going on, he let go of Stormy's cuff chain and dropped his knife in distracted confusion. Wayland and the surviving shifters seized the moment. They charged in a horde, swinging their whips around Thorn's ankles and felling him. Stormy took cover behind a tree. She watched the epic struggle as Wayland, his coyote shifters, and Thorn thrashed around, Thorn bashing them with his metal fists. She cringed at Thorn landing a wicked punch to Wayland's already bloody shoulder and another to his gut.

Wayland regained the upper hand and yanked Thorn's armored head back. Thorn screeched in agony when Wayland repeated the neck jerk, just short of snapping her brother's spine. "I can't pierce your body armor, but I can damn well hogtie you!" Wayland yelled at Thorn, writhing on the ground.

"Here to help," the coyotes roared. They crowded around, offered their whips, and held Thorn down as Wayland used them to add more knots, securing Thorn's arms, legs and neck, and tying him to a tree.

Stormy saw the terror in Thorn's exposed face, his wide eyes. Wayland cursed and paced in front of him, holding back from the kill.

"Stormy, untie me! I'm your brother. I'm sorry I locked you up. I was only trying to protect you," Thorn screeched. "I've always tried to protect you! How can you let this vile pack enemy tie me up?"

Stormy stepped up to Thorn and examined him like he was an insect under her microscope. "You had choices, *brother*. You almost always chose the heartless paths, the vicious actions. I used to love you." She nodded slowly with a passing flicker of wistful regret. "But no more. Your true sadism came out in the last year when you slaughtered the Leblancs, and in these last weeks, when you planned to kill the very last one. I guess your brutality was always there. It frightens me that I had such a blind spot. I don't love you anymore. I don't even pity you, no matter if you're my brother or not."

"Half-brother," Wayland said quietly from beside her. She turned his way and saw him shifting to human, his claws retracting, his animal fur shifting to human skin. His black wavy hair was soaked in sweat, and his emerald eyes gleamed. He strode toward her, every inch of him sending out vibes of passion, respect, and an intense, driving need. She rushed to him and they wrapped their arms around each other, holding on for dear life. God, she could stay like this forever. It was delicious, cosmic, and sexy as hell. "I was so worried about you," she whispered.

"I thought about you every second. I was scared for you, too. You're so thin. You haven't been eating." He pulled her closer. "We need to talk. About us."

"Yes. I want to," she murmured and kissed the vulnerable part of his neck below the jaw, his cheek, and the side of his scarred head where his ear used to be.

"But before anything, you need to decide…about Thorn."

She gazed into his eyes, green pools of wisdom and heart. "What do you think, Wayland?"

He nuzzled her neck, kissed her forehead, then in her ear, he murmured, "It's in your hands, sweet Stormy. I could plunge my fist clear through his face. Every other part of this coward is protected by that stupid armor except for that. I could kill him or…not." He gazed down at her, and then over to Thorn, who perspired so profusely, it ran in rivulets down his wide, pale face.

"Killing him is too kind," she growled.

Yes, killing Thorn is way too kind. I have an idea, said the female voice in her head. *Humiliate him as he has humiliated you. Reduce him and make him servile.*

"Reduce him? Tell me more," Stormy mused out loud to no one in particular. Wayland, who was still holding her, didn't look surprised.

"Who are you talking to?" snapped Thorn. "You sound stark raving mad!" Everyone ignored him.

"I know an old woman in the town where Thorn held me held captive, who is quite lonely. I know what it's like to be lonely." Now, the woman's voice came from outside of Stormy, from somewhere in the woods. The coyote shifters sniffed the air and turned toward the line of pines at the forest's edge.

"The old candlemaker?" asked Wayland, looking that way.

"Yes! The candlemaker you mentioned from Winter Crow. Wayland, you said she longed for a companion."

"A little lap dog," he said, a twinkle in his eye.

"Oh, hell no!" shouted Thorn, struggling to escape his binds.

"How perfect!" Stormy sang. "What brilliant justice. Can your magic turn Thorn into her obedient little lapdog?" she asked the trees.

147

"Yes!" A woman emerged from the pines and seemed to float their way with the two witches from Wayland's neighboring campsite in tow. She wore a crimson gown and a regal wreath of red wildflowers on white hair that flowed down her back. "I'm Eliza, your mother, and you are my beautiful daughter."

"Mama!" Stormy broke out in sobs, as she ran into her mother's arms.

CHAPTER 21

𝒲 ayland

WATCHING THE TWO WOMEN EMBRACE, Wayland was over-joyed. The coyote shifters cheered from the sidelines. Thorn still writhed fruitlessly to loosen the corded knots before his fate was sealed. Wayland quite liked seeing this entitled Tundra turd squiggle like an insect under a flyswatter.

"You've grown up to be such a lovely woman," Eliza cooed, stroking Stormy's coal black hair.

"You're beautiful, too, Mother. I always imagined you as an exotic queen, sitting on a throne, eating plums, and drinking apricot tea." Stormy held her mom at arm's length and smiled. "I did picture your long, snowy hair correctly!"

It struck Wayland how mother and daughter's laughter had a similar melody to it. And they both stood tall, slim and regal.

"It's so much better to see you than dream you," Stormy said.

"During those dark days I tried to talk to you through animals—"

"Yes, I remember. A kitten told me nursery rhymes."

"I embodied the little critter. It was the only way to see you, to talk to you after your father ripped you from my arms. I'm sorry to say he wanted to kill me. Jagger had the cruel streak that Thorn inherited. They wanted to pretend you were pure Tundra and were both willing to kill to perpetuate the lie. But I outsmarted them. I cast a spell that insured Thorn's death if they tried to kill me."

Thorn snarled at this, and everyone looked over in surprise, as if they thought he was already gone.

"Oh, Mama, I'm so sad about what you had to go through. Held in a prison for over twenty years! I could hardly stand being in prison for a week."

"In metal prisons, so neither of you could astral travel," added Wayland. They embraced him and thanked him again for helping them. "It's an honor to help those I care about." He hugged them back and offered bottles of water and venison jerky. Stormy was thin and undoubtedly parched. She drank the water with gusto and nibbled on the dried venison.

"Suze and Jacey helped too," Wayland said. "Suze whirled up some wicked purple mini-tornados for interference."

"And Jacey turned the legs of the Tundra in the lake into stone," Eliza noted. She gestured for the two witches to come close. They eagerly joined the huddle.

"We can spell cast together," Stormy said, "and send Thorn to his final fate. Lapdog! Can you picture it?" The women burst out laughing, and a growing group of recovering coyote shifters joined in. This was spicy and cathartic entertainment after their challenging battle.

The women exchanged stories and more embraces, and Wayland excused himself. He rushed around the lake to where Bones lay, horribly still. For a wrenching moment, Wayland thought he'd departed to the great beyond. But when he kneeled, he was relieved to hear Bones's labored breaths. "Hang in there, bro," Wayland murmured. "Going to get you out of this mess." He reached in his pocket for a bunch of eucalyptus and crunched it in his fist so it would exude its pungent medicine. He held it under Bones's nose. "Breathe in."

Bones inhaled slowly at first, and then another time, longer and deeper. His eyes flickered open. "Wayland. Did you get the bastard?"

"I did, with your help!" Wayland wasn't the crying type, but tears filled his eyes.

"A lot of help I was, stuck in this infernal swamp," Bones muttered, and tried to lift his shoulders. The intense suction of the mud glued him there. "I can't even move!"

"Here. Grab on." Bones took Wayland's hands, and Wayland slowly pulled him up, after sticking his boot between Bones and the mud to release the suction. Bones sat up with a juicy *ploop*.

Wayland took the hooch from his pocket and gave Bones a drink, along with some potion the coyote she-healers had given him. It did the trick, and the fact that shifters healed three times as quickly as humans. Wayland's arm wound was also closing. The place where his ear was had already knit itself together.

Around the lake, he saw coyote shifters rise in the same way. A few Tundra, too, who were quickly rounded up and secured for questioning.

Wayland wasn't so bloodthirsty as to kill every Tundra shifter. He would interrogate each one and make a thoughtful assessment. Sabine's murder did not justify the murder of an entire pack, even the Tundra.

Only the intractable ones who still insist Thorn is a god.

The next wave of activity involved the coyote women, accompanied by Red Claw. He led the procession, still wearing his theatrical raven-feather headdress. *Hoo yowl* they howled, and *Yee yip yip*, which Wayland remembered from lessons at the coyote den meant *Victory!*

"Yee yip yip he howled in response.

The shifter females spread around the lake, attending to their coyote mates and helping each other pull them from the muddy banks as Wayland had helped Bones. Bones's mate, Berry, was beside herself with joy, bending over Bones and kissing him. It touched Wayland and he hoped he could win Stormy's heart and be as happy with her as Bones was with Berry after so many years together.

Wayland thanked Red Claw for his clever car heist. "My pleasure!" Red Claw exclaimed, pulling Suze into his arms. "That ATV burns some badass rubber!" He gave Suze another lusty squeeze. "Hey, sexy lady, want to burn more rubber with me in that hot rod?"

"Hell yasss!" she shouted, pumping her arm in solidarity.

"But first, we have spell casting to do, right Wayland?" Suze gave Wayland a wink.

"You witches will put on the best show of the century!" he said. "Bring out the popcorn!"

Stormy and Eliza motioned them over. It was time. Wayland's gut flipped in anticipation of the spell, but also for what would follow: his talk with Stormy. He had a lot to say to her. And he was sure she had a lot to say, too. He could hardly wait.

The witches gathered around. Stormy drew a small pentagram near Thorn and helped Eliza light the bundles of herbs they'd carried there. Suze spread salt on strategic power points. Jacey recited the first prayer to Hecate.

Stormy and Eliza held hands and recited the spell, almost perfectly in sync, like they had practiced it a dozen times and were not just instantaneously reading each other's minds.

Goddess of magic, stars, and the moon,
We ask you a favor on this night of June,
To change Thorn into a docile lapdog,
And send him through night and snow and fog,
To the Candlemaker up in Winter Crow,
To be her companion forever. Now go!

Thorn, who had been alternately writhing and cursing, got somber. "No, no, no, no," he groaned as they finished the chant.

Wayland could swear he saw the moon in the darkening sky flicker on, off, and then on like some cosmic light switch. Others stared at it, too.

When they looked back at Thorn, he was gone.

* * *

THE CANDLEMAKER

In Winter Crow, the snow outside the candlemaker's windows was relentless, driving almost sideways from the fierce winds. She feared the blizzards on Candle Lane. It meant being snowed in for weeks, all alone.

She sighed. She had her candles to make, and the fireplace to warm her bent arthritic bones, and even a cupboard of beans and rice and soup. But there was no one to talk to. Hardly a soul was left in the town since the exodus after the Blue Fevers ten years back. There was no one to check on her since her only son had died from it.

She wondered how much longer she'd live. She was eighty-eight. Her mother had lived to a hardy hundred and three. That was fifteen more years if her calculations were right. Long and lonely years.

She leaned back into her tattered easy chair and gazed at

the flickering fire. Suddenly, it billowed into a blue whorl, then stifled down almost to nothing.

An unexpected burst of wind blasted through the room. Was a window open? Or had the force of the blizzard broken a panel of glass? She'd better check. Once the heat escaped, her house could become a perilous refrigerator in no time. When she reached for her cane, she was startled so thoroughly she almost keeled over. A small dog had suddenly appeared on her footstool. He yipped, scurried into her lap and curled into a contented ball.

The pup had soft gray and white fur with dark round eyes. Where in the world had this wondrous gift come from? It was baffling, but who was she to complain? She eased back, reached out a hand and scratched the little tyke between its ears.

CHAPTER 22

S tormy

FINALLY, she and Wayland were alone. Eliza, Suze, and Jacey had gone back to Snow Mountain Lodge and the coyote shifters went to their den. They would meet with the coyotes in a day or two, and with Eliza and the witches for a late dinner at the hotel.

Even after all she and Wayland had been through, Stormy found herself shuffling her feet and stealing shy peeks at him like a schoolgirl. His black hair was tangled and sweaty, his bare chest was lined with bloody claw marks already knitting together. Her attraction to him was magnetic; his scent of masculine musk was irresistible.

"Come with me?" he asked and reached for her hand. She gladly took it. It was electric and strong and reassuring. They walked to a secluded part of the forest, near the old Leblanc den, where the blackberry brambles circled around a small, hidden glen. The moonlight cast a dewy, amber glow on their faces. They stood gazing at each other and holding both hands now. She could look into his forest green eyes for days. "I don't care that you're half Tundra, and I love that you're half witch," he murmured. "You're the smartest, bravest woman I've ever met."

"Thanks, Wayland. You believed in me when I didn't believe in myself. You fought to be with me when I was afraid and unsure. You were patient and kind even when I was testy and giving you a hard time." She brushed back a lock of his hair that had drifted over his eye. "You were daring in seeking out my lost mother, freeing her and returning her safely. You were fearless in fighting my brother's devilish evil. I'm ashamed of him, and of how I stayed connected to him for way too long, I—"

"Don't be embarrassed. It took you some time. You had to overcome your fear, and the intense brainwashing he put you through for years. No one should push another person to change. You are worth waiting for." He kissed her tenderly on the forehead. She so wanted more, but this coming together would play out organically, as Wayland said, without either of them rushing this part.

"Do you still think about Sabine?" She couldn't help asking.

"Sometimes, but not as a lover, not with a broken heart any more. I used to think that I was damaged goods. That love was only for other people, no longer for me."

Oh, blessed heart! "I understand, Wayland, I do. I disliked my life, being taught to hate everyone who wasn't in our so-called morally pure circle, being told that the outside world was dangerous, and I needed protection. Ha! It took me so long to see that I was the one who was trapped—in a Tundra prison of Thorn's making."

"Sweet, sweet Stormy..." Wayland released her hands and

sank down on one knee. *Is he...? Is he really?* Her heart beat so hard against her ribs she thought she might pass out.

He took one of her hands again and rubbed her palm with his thumb. "I've loved you for so many years."

Oh yes, he is!

She understood, suddenly, the Victorian term swooning. Granted, she hadn't eaten in days, and she was faint. But this was so much more profound. "I've had a crush on you since I was a little girl," she admitted. "I love you, too."

Her words softened his jaw and shoulders. He leaned closer, and his mouth upturned in a perilously sexy grin. "And so, dear Stormy, I want to ask for your hand in marriage. Be my mate. If you'll have me, a flawed but well-intentioned guy."

Oh, blessed moon goddess.

On top of being faint, now she was trembling. "Yes! I'd love it. Yes!" She sank onto her knees to meet his lips. He wrapped her in his arms, and they tumbled down in the bramble and kissed again.

CHAPTER 23

W ayland

PRECIOUS LOVE, precious lady. My heart. My soul.

He ran his hands along her silky curves, lingering at the swell of her hips, then worked around to her wide, luscious ass. As she bucked up to meet the push of his palms on her nether cheeks, he humped her through her pants and pressed his erection firmly enough to make it clear how much she'd excited him.

She tore at his jeans button, and he fumbled with hers. They wriggled free of clothes, and he wasted no time finding her firm nipples and sucking them, one after the other. He inhaled her scent of phlox and woodsy earth. His hand meandered down to the juicy paradise between her legs and he fingered his way into the ruffled lips and settled on her throbbing clit. He went at it playfully at first, then faster, with intentional pressure as he felt himself edging closer to his own peak.

She moaned and put her hands all over him—his ribs, his broad shoulders, clawing his back, then goosing his ass. Her hands moved to his groin, and they both moaned when she clasped his hard length and stroked it.

"Let's make a baby," she whispered in his ear.

He almost came at hearing this. My god, she was ballsy, fearless, faster than lightning. "Are you sure, Stormy?"

She nipped his ear hard. Breathed her brand of fire into it. "I'm sure. Let's keep your royal status. Let's win that damn bet."

He pulled away and frowned at her. "It's not about that, Stormy."

"I know. I know, Wayland." She nipped his nose and bit his neck. "I'm halfway joking. But hell, we'll make the best wolf baby in the universe, and it will be surrounded by love, so why the hell not, and we're getting married, and *day-um*, just go ahead and fuck me hard, Mr. Badass Hubby-to-be!"

"We *will* make great parents." He bit her lightly on the mouth and rolled his tongue slowly around each lip. "You *are* my fated mate, Stormy. I love you beyond all reason and time." He drew his tongue along her neck and down one arm until she mewled. "And your hips are incredibly beautiful baby-making hips, Mrs. Royal Wolf Queen Wifey-to be, so let's do this thing!"

With that, he went at it in full wolfish style, taking her fiercely, and they fucked like mad until they came together in a chorus of ecstatic howls that graced the night.

 tormy

"CELESTINE, SWEET FOREST BABY," cooed Stormy, as she sat in her favorite chair and rocked the wee one, who already had fetching black curls at three months old. Stormy and Wayland had nabbed the rocker in a Louisiana vintage market the day they learned she was pregnant. It had wooden carvings of moons and suns on the headrest and gentle scrolls running along each armrest. It had called out to them, *'I'm yours! Take me!'*

Celestine drooled and giggled at Stormy and waggled her toes in the purple booties Granny Eliza had made. "Woo!" she burbled.

"Woo! Howwwl!" Stormy howled back, which sent Celestine's feet bicycling like mad.

"It isn't hard to amuse her," Eliza noted from where she sat by the window, its sill brimming with pots of blue phlox and herbs and delicate white balloon flowers. "She already sounds like a tiny she-wolf." The two women chuckled.

"Hey, she was forged in the bramble, so it makes perfect sense. I'll never forget, the night we made her, we gazed up into the night sky and thought of baby names."

"Tell me again, Stormy. I never get tired of hearing it," said Eliza, petting her old dog, Knight, who she had conjured back with her staff and a spell months ago.

"Well, Celestine's the name of a crystalline mineral stone with a blue tint, and Wayland says it reminds him of my Tundra eyes." Stormy winked at her mom. "Oh, before that we thought of Bramble if it was a boy, and Lake if it was a girl." She looked down at her baby girl, still making *woo* sounds. "But Celestine just fits!" Eliza nodded.

Stormy was grateful to have her mother here to help watch Celestine, but who knew Eliza would also be a master window gardener, and start a coven in a matter of weeks, enticing a handful of Louisiana territory's most clever and fervent witches to join? Not to mention Eliza functioned in her priestess role and had married them the day after that battle at Ice Lake. Eliza was sure making up for all that lost time in *Winter fucking Crow*, as Wayland liked to put it.

Stormy breastfed the baby and looked around the room. It was almost a feat of magic the way they transformed it from the rat hole Wayland had brought them to about a year ago. The place had been piled with unpacked boxes, dishes in the sink, and dust balls everywhere. He'd explained, reddening with embarrassment, that he'd been in a funk, and it was all he could do to get up in the morning and feed himself. Stormy, Eliza, and Wayland had all worked hard to scrub the place and unpack Wayland's boxes plus their own suitcases from Canada. They'd purchased new furniture, and Eliza designed a lovely sanctuary of her own in Wayland's spare room with crimson drapes, a velvet couch, and pillows in the mysterious, moody style she was partial to. Wayland bought Stormy and himself a king bed and silk sheets, the better to roll around on. They'd decked out the place with sexy vintage poster prints of the bayou and trees draped in Spanish lace.

Now that she was full of warm milk, Celestine rubbed her sleepy eyes. Stormy zipped her dress top and adjusted it. She was excited to go out on the town with Wayland. Date night with the hubby!

Wayland walked in and over to Stormy. She glanced up admiringly at him. "You've gone all out, Mr. Leblanc. You look dashing in your oyster gray suit."

"You look gorgeous yourself, Mrs. Leblanc." He leaned over and kissed her, while brushing a hand over Celestine's dark curls. "My lord, are you trying to bewitch me all over again in that red dress and those flowers in your hair?" He raised a cryptic brow. "If so, bewitch away!"

Eliza rose from her chair and gently took the already sleeping Celestine in her arms. "You two go out and have a fabulous time."

Stormy got up and kissed her mother on the cheek. "Thanks, Mom, we will."

CHAPTER 25

$\mathcal{W}$ayland

HE PAUSED in the downstairs foyer to pull Stormy in and give her a long, fervent kiss. He thrust his tongue in her mouth as a preview of something else he would thrust into her later. She moaned and bit his neck.

"I have a very special evening planned," he revealed.

"I can't wait!" she gushed. "I love surprises."

It was the anniversary of the epic battle, of Thorn's hilarious transformation, of their marriage, and of Celestine's conception in the hidden glen of the bramble. Stormy, Wayland and Eliza all agreed the stars were aligned during those June days, so no longer were Stormy and Wayland star-crossed lovers. The heavens themselves had juggled things around in their favor.

Wayland held the door for Stormy, and inhaled as she walked by, her phlox perfume inflaming his lust, and they hadn't even eaten dinner yet.

"Good evening, Nola Jaye," Stormy said to the old turbaned fortuneteller, a fixture on the apartment complex's front bench.

"Why, hello. Don't you two look like the bobcat's whiskers?" Nola Jaye chirped, her face wrinkling into a myriad of laugh lines. She picked up her Tarot deck and fanned it out. "A card for the evening?"

"Sure." Stormy closed her eyes and ran her hand just above them, like she was divining water—or pure gold. Her hand lowered and she plucked one from the left side.

Nola Jaye chuckled. "The Queen of Hearts! My, my, love fit for a queen. You're going to have quite a celebration tonight, Mrs. Leblanc."

"Yep. One fantastic time," Wayland agreed, pulling Stormy into a hug.

"No clues!" Stormy said. "Keep the surprise!"

Wayland made a zipping motion across his grinning mouth, but it was hard to keep the secret. He opened the car door for his lovely wife.

Wayland had rented the same minicamper he'd had in Canada and parked it in a picturesque spot on the nearby Red River. He'd sprinkled the floor with blue forest phlox and spread silk sheets on the bed. They could have wild sex all night without the baby crying, or Eliza overhearing them scream and howl in the throes of passion.

Yes, they would have a hot, hot time, and yes, Stormy was the witch queen to his alpha king.

The End

Want even more Royal Alpha Wolves? Make sure you read the whole series to find out if the royal bloodlines continue with Alec, Wayland and Tobias. Read in any order!

The Royal Alpha Wolves Club Series

4 books. 4 authors. 4 alphas. 1 shared world.

Bella Night – Bound by Blood (Book 1: Dorian's story)

R.J. Lloyd – Heir to Redemption (Book 2: Alec's story)

Catherine Stine – Alpha's Revenge (Book 3: Wayland's story)

M.R. Polish – Savage Vengeance (Book 4: Tobias's story)

* * *

HERE'S a sneak peek of the next book in the series:

Savage Vengeance by M. R. Polish

Prologue – Tobias's story

"Well, things could've gone worse." Tobias chuckled as he helped Ellis pick up the last of the splintered bar furniture.

The surly bar owner glared at him. "I wouldn't be so sure about that."

"What do you mean?" Tobias asked. "The place is still standing." He gave his friend a sly smile.

"Barely," Ellis grumbled.

"Oh, come on. How long have we been putting the Lazy Moon back together? We've seen much worse. Hell, we've done much worse," Tobias teased, remembering the good old days when he and Ellis used to run wild with the wolves of the Louisiana territory.

He often missed those carefree days. Being the head of the Royal Alpha Wolves Club wasn't a job he'd ever wanted. But, he supposed that's what made him so good at it.

He was fair and just. And that's what the shifters needed most at the moment. There had been too much violence and corruption in the past. It was time someone stopped it. And if it had to be him, then so be it.

His family wasn't happy about it, but with shifter numbers dwindling to an all-time low, even they understood something must be done.

"Well," Tobias said, shrugging on his jacket. "I'd better get going."

"What? You're not gonna stay for a beer?" Ellis teased. "I guess being head honcho means you're too good to slum it with your old pal, huh?"

"Never," Tobias winked. "But you know Ava will kill me if I'm late for dinner."

Ellis gave a raspy laugh. "If the Club only knew it was really your mate who wears the pants in your pack now."

"Yeah, yeah. I'll give her your love, Ellis."

"Actually, I don't think you will," purred a deep voice with a thick accent.

Tobias turned to see Caz Desmond and his pack standing in the open door of the Lazy Moon. Representing all the wolves of Brazil, Caz held a great deal of power and he knew it. He was most likely here to negotiate more lenient terms for his pack.

Tobias had anticipated that Caz would be one of the most difficult delegations to win over, but he couldn't start making exceptions now. Even for a man as powerful as Caz. But he knew he'd have to handle this situation with care.

Taking a deep breath, Tobias rallied all the patience and diplomacy he had left. "Caz, how can I help you?"

"It is you, I fear, who is in need of help," Caz replied.

"What?"

Caz snapped his fingers and a group of his men dragged a female wolf forward. She was chained and her copper coat was matted with blood. "Please, I'll do anything. Just let her go."

Caz grinned wickedly. "I know you will. But this is just business. What do you call it, an insurance policy? You understand."

Tobias met his mate's fierce green eyes one last time before Caz's pack dragged her away. There was fear in Ava's eyes, but she nodded anyway, trying to spare Tobias any further pain.

How would he survive without her?

The wolf inside him snarled, with fury. He would get her back, no matter the cost.

ABOUT THE AUTHOR

Catherine Stine is a *USA Today* bestselling author of historical fantasy, paranormal romance and sci-fi thrillers. Witch of the Wild Beasts won a second prize spot in the '19 RWA Sheila Contest. Other novels have earned Indie Notable awards and New York Public Library Best Books for Teens. She lives in Manhattan, grew up in Philadelphia and is known to roam the Catskills. Before writing novels, she was a painter and children's fabric designer. She's a visual author when it comes to scenes, and she sees writing as painting with words. She loves edgy thrills, perhaps because her dad read Edgar Allen Poe tales to her as a child. Catherine loves spending time with her beagle Benny, writing about supernatural creatures, gardening on her deck, traveling and meeting readers at book fests.

OTHER BOOKS BY CATHERINE

Witch of the Wild Beasts

Witch of the Cards

Pictures of Dorianna

Fireseed One

Ruby's Fire

Want news of her new books, sales and appearances?

Sign up for her mailing list here.